HELEN

ENOUGH IS NOT ENOUGH

RICHARD LEE

*Dedicated to a world in need of
love and imagination.*

"Too much of a good thing can be wonderful!"

- Mae West

FOREWORD

The EROS CRESCENT novels take you on a journey like no other - to places you couldn't imagine - a female friendly sex club or a privately owned members-only dogging venue; the toy-boy life of a writer working on the Amalfi coast and much much more. *HELEN* and the other novellas - *JESSICA, MARIA, JANICE, MARY* and *THE CLUB* - are extracts taken from *The Fifi Code, Eros Crescent* and *Mount Eros*. All are available as Kindle ebooks or as paperbacks at Amazon.com

PREFACE

The two bodies clasped each other tightly and tongued each other and Helen's body shook regularly with tiny orgasms that it was prone to do when excitement overwhelmed her, and which she hadn't experienced for a very long time.

— *from Mount Eros*

1

HELEN

HELEN ARRIVED on time and Alice invited her to over to the flat where she was studying. She had prepared nibbles and had the coffee machine set to go.

They embraced and kissed each other on the cheek and settled down, Helen on the sofa and Alice in the big easy chair opposite. She was genuinely pleased to see this lovely woman, and she appeared to feel the same way about seeing me.

"Well, Helen. I'm wondering what brings you here. There seems to be a hint of mystery somewhere. Has Frederico been beating you?"

They both laughed. Freddy was notoriously kind and thoughtful, the sort of man who caught moths or spiders in the house, and carefully escorted them out the back door. The idea of him lifting a hand in anger was unthinkable. Now that I thought about it, there were moments in my early teens when I had a sort of crush on my stepfather, and I was adamant that I would one day find a man just like him.

"Well, he hasn't yet. You most of all, Alice, know how thoughtful and considerate he is."

"Indeed I do. I can confess to you now that before I got my first boyfriend, I had decided that when I grew up I would find a man just like Freddy."

We both laughed.

There was a sudden quiet moment, and I could see that Helen was showing signs of unease.

"Is everything all right, Helen? Are you worried about something."

Helen's face changed and she looked more relaxed.

"Worried is not quite how I would put it, but I do have a little problem, Alice, and I have an idea you might be able to help."

"Oh! Now I'm really worried. Tell me about it, Helen."

I was taken with Helen's lovely green-painted leather low-heeled sandals with the small coloured wooden bead decoration. Her shapely and attractive bare legs were crossed and she rotated her foot first one way then the other. I had to make myself look away. I realised that she had observed me observing her and I tried really hard not to blush.

"I spent some time with Rosa last week. We had a very deep and meaningful discussion, and she opened up and told me a lot about her and Bertie's relationship. She mentioned that you knew that I had lived with a woman, and that you were very accepting of it. Later I thought about that and decided you were the person I should be talking to in fact, particularly you."

Helen paused and looked a little uncomfortable.

"Please come over here and sit beside me, Alice. It feels like I'm at the doctor's or something, with you way over there."

I went and sat beside her. She was obviously agitated and having trouble working out how to tell me something, so I took her hand. She squeezed it appreciatively.

"I am hoping that you will understand what I'm about to say. But firstly I should mention something that I remembered you saying the night of Frederico's birthday party last year.

I giggled. "Oh Helen, I was a little tiddly that night. I hope I didn't say anything offensive, or embarrass anyone?"

She laughed a more relaxed laugh.

"No, Alice you actually said something that gave me strength."

"I did? Please tell me more."

"We met in the passageway near the kitchen, where a doorway leads off to the laundry and the driveway. I was standing waiting for a friend, who had gone out to their car, to come back in.

"You came along, slightly unsteady on your feet. You uncharacteristically put an arm around my waist and put your face up close to mine and said, 'You are so beautiful. If only I had the courage to swing both ways.' Then you took your arm back and wandered off."

"Oh my God, Helen, did I really do that? I don't remember any of it. Are you sure it was me?"

She giggled at my embarrassment. I looked at her face. She was smiling and her eyes sparkled and she looked at me intently. Helen lifted up her legs and crossed them the other way and suddenly her other foot was turning and moving provocatively.

"Yes, you did and you made my heart soar. I needed to have more courage in my life, and the strength to do what I really wanted to do. Which brings me to the reason why I am here. I just pray you will understand, and bear with me till I finish."

I squeezed her hand and nodded an assurance.

"I have desperately missed the sort of love I once had with women friends. I love Freddy dearly, and he is a wonderful lover, but it doesn't stop me having this half-empty feeling deep down. But I cannot deceive Frederico. I cannot have a secret lover. It would destroy me and us. So I've thought of a plan to involve him in a loving, sharing arrangement. And this is where I need your help, Alice."

She stopped talking and looked at me to see if I was hearing her, and understanding what she was saying and I sensed that she was feeling awkward and acting like an adolescent in love.

She was about to go on but I spoke first.

"Helen, if you will let me kiss you on the lips first, the rest might become a little easier than you think."

The look on Helen's face was one of incredulousness followed by a surprised happiness that shone like a light.

Before I could move towards her she had thrown herself onto me and our lips became glued and stayed glued seemingly for ever. Then I slowly offered her my tongue and she trembled and met my tongue with hers. When we finally pulled away, we sat looking happily into each others eye's.

"Helen darling, I hereby declare me as your first new lady lover. Please say you accept me as that?"

"Yes, yes, yes, sweet Alice, I accept you as my lover with all my heart."

We kissed again then I moved her back to where she was first sitting.

"Now my new love, tell me your plan for getting over the Freddy problem."

But Helen didn't want to do that straight away. She had other ideas.

"At this moment Alice, I only want one thing, and that is you. Please allow me to touch you. I have been so empty for so long. Suddenly, I want to feel a love that only you can give me."

She reached over and began to unbutton my blouse, and I began to drag her top up from inside her skirt. We were both braless and in just moments we were bare-breasted.

We alternated between kissing each other on the lips, each caressing the other's neck kissing each other's breasts and gently biting each other's nipples. I swung my leg over her, and kneeled facing her. We cupped each others breasts in our hands and rubbed them against our own. Then I stood up, and taking Helen by the hand, led her to the bedroom.

"I want to take all your clothes off, Helen, and mine too."

For the next hour or more we cavorted naked, every which way, on the big bed and sometimes on the floor or in the armchair beside the bed. We laughed and we sobbed.

Sometimes the enormity of Helen's long isolation from other women overwhelmed her and she cried like a child. And when she had cried enough, I would slap her on the bottom, and tell her that I so wanted to spank her hard but now wasn't the time. She laughed out loud.

"Oh the times I've ached for a good spanking. Make it your number one task, my darling, when next we are together."

We exhausted ourselves, but still couldn't stop wanting more of each other. And when we thought we'd done enough, one or the other would round onto her knees, and push her bottom and pussy towards the other's face and wriggle, midst peals of laughter and licking.

Our first encounter was a truly beautiful time, and we would forever cherish the memory.

"So part two of the story, Helen, is what to do about Freddy and how I might help you with that."

We had dressed, and were back in the lounge having reheated coffee that we had abandoned earlier.

"So I'll not beat about the bush, Alice. I would like you to sleep with your stepdad. And before you list all the reasons why it's not possible, let me ask you: was there ever a time when you all lived together that you fancied Frederico, or perhaps had fantasies about having him as a lover?"

"Oh, Helen, what a dilemma. Yes, of course I had a crush on Freddy, probably within a few months of him getting together with Mum.

"As I got to know him, and stopped being angry with him for having stolen my mother from me, I caved in, and from then on hung on his every word. He sensed my interest and handled me with the utmost care.

"I remember, at around age sixteen, deliberately not locking the bathroom door, running down the hallway naked when I thought he was about to come along, and hitching my school skirt up high when I came home and I knew Mum would still be at work, and he would be alone in the study.

"Nothing ever worked. He was just bloody perfect."

She laughed loudly.

"Just as he is now."

"Are you saying what I think you are saying Helen? That you would like me as your lover and you want to share me with your husband? And this could be the easiest path to follow, given he already knows me? And it will give you peace of mind, and the freedom you want? So are you only here to fix your problem, and I just happen to be a part of the package?"

Helen looked horrified.

"Alice! No! You are the woman I have most ached for, for a very long time. You could just as easily say that I only want to share you with Freddy, so that I can have you as my lover."

We fell silent for quite a long time.

"Freddy, has occasionally mentioned you with great affection. Despite what we might think about him, I know for sure that you have not gone unnoticed, and he has feelings deep down, like most men, that he will not allow himself to admit. And I believe that, understandably, he would have hidden any of these feelings or fantasies in deference to his love for your mother.

"Now that his world has changed and we are together and alone, I believe it would be a healthy thing if he put some of those taboos aside, just as you and I have done today."

We fell silent again. Then I mentioned the Bennetts, and Rosa and Bertie's happy marriage, and how things changed for both of them when Rosa admitted to herself that she needed female love as well as Bertie's love.

"Bertie's research into early Chinese philosophy relating to the increased health and happiness of people who love more than one person, might be the key to all this.

"And yes, dearest Helen, I would go to bed with your husband, and yes, for mostly selfish reasons, one being that I get to have his wife as a lover. If, then, he and I grew closer through our lovemaking, so be it. And if Bertie happened to hear about us, he would rejoice and say that we all were better off because if it."

Helen reached out and took my hand and I leant over and kissed her.

"I think that Rosa and Bertie are the ones who might more easily influence Frederico, and however successful or not a would-be seducer might be, I think a direct approach at this point would not work.

"Does Rosa have an inkling of what you have in mind, Helen?"

"Yes, darling, our conversation was thorough and far-reaching."

Helen gave a funny little smile that made me curious.

"Rosa was very happy that you are looking after Bertie so well."

Helen watched as I coloured up in the deepest possible fit of blushing, and she smiled.

"My God, you're a sexy little bitch. Come here."

Helen pushed me off the sofa and on to the floor and lay on top of me.

We just stayed there lovingly grinding our pussies together and with our mouths glued and our tongues wildly thrashing about inside each other's mouths.

There was much sighing and moaning, as we expressed our delight in having discovered each other at long last. Finally Alice whispered in a mock child's voice.

"And Mummy dearest?"

"Yes, darling?"

"You are the most sexy wicked stepmother ever."

I was happy with the way things were. Freya and I were as passionate about one another as we'd ever been, and Helen continued to be my delightful wicked stepmother.

There was a tiny moment when things involving both of them looked as though they might go awry.

I had told Helen very early in the piece about my loving relationship with Freya. But it wasn't until a few weeks after Helen and I first made love that she brought up the subject of other relationships.

"Alice! I've got this nagging problem with us. You will think I'm being childish I know, but I've realised that I'm feeling jealous of Freya."

"Oh Helen, that's awful. You know that I love you very, very much. And you are always the first to acknowledge that we can love more than one person. You must not be jealous, sweetheart. We must fix this."

Helen stared at her feet and her shoulders were drooped sadly. I sat beside her and held her hand.

"I know I shouldn't be, darling, but it niggles at me. What can I do?"

"Whatever it takes, we'll do it together. I do have one idea which I've wanted to suggest, but thought it might be too soon."

"What is that idea, darling? Please tell me."

I paused for a moment then told her my idea, with my fingers crossed that she wouldn't get upset.

"I feel that you are now as much a part of me as Freya is, and increasingly I want to share you both with each other. I feel that we would benefit by including the three of us in our lovemaking.

"I believe, too, that if I'm not mistaken, you and Freya will fall in love in the same way as the two of us did. If that happens, bingo, jealousy goes out the window. And, there is another thing, your desire to be open and honest with Freddy. I know you would have no trouble finding other lovers. However, you might not want Frederico to think you had been secretly looking out for them. My solution would involve me bringing and introducing Freya to the two of you.

"Bringing Freya to dinner on a Saturday evening and seeing how the two of you reacted to her, and her to you, would be a start."

By this time, Helen was staring at me, obviously interested. Then her face took on that seductive and mischievous smile.

"Is she really tall and thin with tiny breasts?"

I had obviously broken through, and Helen was responding genuinely and with humour.

I reached out and pulled her face to mine with one hand, while the other hand tippy toed up under her skirt. She wriggled in anticipation and pushed her lower half down into the sofa and forward. Our passionate kissing session hinted that we might have just sorted the jealousy problem.

"Yes, Helen, she is a delight. Now, why am I thinking that maybe I'm the one that will end up getting jealous?"

When Alice had left Freya and Helen alone, it didn't take the two of them long to find each other. Helen asked Freya if she would like to see the fish pond with its newly installed lighting.

"It is quite beautiful in the dark."

"Love to Helen. Show me the way."

Almost before the two even reached the pond they began touching each other, tentatively putting their hands around each other's waists and rubbing their fingertips innocently on each other's backsides.

Moments later, Helen backed Freya against the door of her painting studio and kissed her passionately. Freya hung back a tiny bit, anticipating and looking forward to the onslaught of Helen's obviously strong desire for her.

But she wasn't expecting Helen's next move. Helen pulled her forward and swung her round to face the door. Then the seducer pulled up Freya's skirt.

Helen had wanted to see and touch Freya's extraordinary long thin legs and tiny buttocks from the first moment she had met her. Now there was nothing to stop her

Helen moaned with pleasure as she discovered the gentle Freya's delightful big silk knickerbockers, her latest fashion statement. Helen slipped her hand first up one leg and dragged the knicker leg up to expose the full length of Freya's beautiful leg, then she pulled down the waist to find the tiny bottom, and put her hand on it. She shivered and felt wet between her legs.

Helen's lust was potent. She was wildly excited and Freya appreciated it, joyfully sharing in the lustful anticipation.

Freya found the door handle and turned it, and went into the studio. Helen followed and guided her towards a sofa bed, just made visible by the lights of the fish pond shining through the window.

Freya turned to face Helen.

"I want you to make love to me, Helen and I desperately want you to take you clothes off and for me to lie on your naked body and shag you. I will undress you while you do what you want to do. I want you to touch me everywhere, Helen."

Helen sighed and began to undress Freya. It didn't take long. A skirt and a blouse, a tiny bra and her bloomers all came off, leaving her in her socks and her little white sandals.

And while Freya slipped Helen's dress over her head, then stopped to stare at her beautiful breasts, Helen vented her lust on Freya's tiny breasts and nipples. And when Helen paused for breath, Freya pushed Helen down on the bed and spread herself on top of her and with their mouths joined, she shagged her seducer to their first orgasms together.

"Oh my God, Freya, you are such a beautiful woman. I will want to make love to you again and again."

"Please let's do that Helen. I will want much more of you, too."

———

It was only a few weeks after Helen had played Good Samaritan and handed keys to the potting shed to Mary so that she and Charlie could meet to make love in secret, that Helen, passing the potting shed on her way to her studio, heard a muffled sound coming from within. It didn't sound like a couple making love; rather more like someone sobbing.

Helen stopped and wondered if she should investigate. If there was something going on between lovers, that was their affair, and she should not interfere. But she could hear only one person, and decided to knock and enter.

"Mary? Are you all right, darling?"

She heard Mary blow her nose and then, a few moments later, call out for her to come in.

Mary sat looking gorgeous as only she could, her weight pushing out her stockings, her dress and blouse in Rubenesque splendour, and everything designed to precariously balance on her strappy high heels.

"Darling Mary? What is wrong? Tell me?"

Mary said nothing, but simply passed her phone to Helen. Helen read the message:

So sorry my darling, Hilda has found out and is fearful of a scandal. We are already on a plane heading for an extended holiday on a cruise ship in Europe. She has arranged for number nineteen to be sold immediately we get back. Will be in touch. Much love, Charlie.

"Oh, Mary, you poor darling."

I sat on the bed beside her and wrapped my arms around the large lady. I could feel her shaking with emotion.

We must have sat like that for a good half hour, until Mary could cry no more.

Suddenly she gave a short little laugh.

"Well, Charlie gets a holiday in Europe out of it."

I giggled in response.

"But Mary, that is not what Charlie really wants. He wants to be here in your arms."

That opened the floodgates again.

When Mary had once again become silent, we just sat. Then I adjusted us both to be more comfortable and we lounged back against the pillows stacked against the wall behind us.

"I will especially miss the kissing," Mary squeaked.

After a few minutes of silence, I spoke.

"I think we could possible fix that. Well, sort of."

"What do you mean, Helen?"

I had one arm around her neck and my other arm and hand rested on her large thigh. Then I gently turned the hand over and began to rub her thigh through her skirt.

I drew Mary's head towards mine, and, lifting my hand from her thigh, I turned her face towards me. Mary's still wet eyes focused on my face and I smiled lovingly at her. Then I put my lips on hers, knowing that this could be a terrible mistake.

I left my lips on hers. She didn't immediately respond, but at least she hadn't pulled away.

I was ready to retreat and remove my lips, when suddenly Mary pushed back at me with her mouth, gently. I waited a moment, wanting to give her some space. Then she pushed at me harder.

I put my hand behind her head and pulled it slowly towards me while increasing the pressure on her lips. Then I took a risk and pushed my tongue into her mouth, just a tiny distance, and moved it slowly, side to side.

All of her body shook and as it subsided, I realised that Mary was experiencing a huge emotional release. But there must still have been some tension remaining. I could feel her looking for something, something more, looking for what I might do next.

I decided to take another risk.

I unbuttoned my blouse. I was without a bra and I felt the cool air on my breasts. I picked up Mary's right hand and slowly placed it inside my blouse and waited.

I felt Mary shaking and gasping as she hurriedly moved her hand around, feeling my skin and discovering a nipple. And while she was doing that, she picked up my spare hand and placed it against the exposed skin of her large bosom, and I gratefully slid my hand down inside her top. I too found a nipple and I too, gasped and sighed.

Then Mary began to moan and moved her mouth around on mine, and we both tongued each other.

"I want to help you get through this, Mary my darling. Please let me make love to you?"

I only had to wait a second or two before she answered.

"Oh yes, Helen, please, please make love to me. This all feels so wonderful, so right. Do whatever you want to me, Helen. Anything!"

I held her tight. Then I asked her to follow me to my studio just a few metres away, where we would be much more comfortable.

We stood up and moved to the studio.

We lay down on the big bed and made ourselves comfortable. Mary was desperate to keep kissing me and pawed at me to get to my lips. And when I let her, and our mouths were again fastened together, and we had each resumed our nipple play, I slowly moved my hand down to her crotch and lightly fingered her through her skirt.

"Oh Helen, this is heavenly," Mary whispered.

She reached down and drew up her skirt, then she took my hand and pushed it down into her knickers, placing it atop her huge pouting hairy pussy. We both gave an excited cry.

"Oh yes, Mary! That feels so good. Thank you, my darling."

"Helen, it belongs to you now. Your fingers feel wonderful. Do anything, darling. Whatever you want, and I will love and cherish you for it always."

I lifted my head and gazed down on Mary's enormous stockinged thighs and legs. Her suspenders rolled down and over her fleshy upper thigh, on their way to her stocking tops.

I knew what I wanted next. It was something that my true love, Alice and I shared a lust for: seeing a woman's stockinged legs and shoes waving in the air.

Holding Mary's legs up in the air and looking at them, while I shafted her with the big strap-on, hidden beneath the bed, would be so wonderful and sexy. And I believed Mary would enjoy it too.

As we kissed and I slowly rotated my hand on Mary's pussy, I reached down and brought out the strap-on from beneath the bed. I did not want to frighten her with it, so I knew she had to see it first.

"Mary darling, I've got a special thing that Frederico and I play with sometimes if he's feeling a little flat and I need his attention. Would you like to see it?"

Mary looked at me quizzically.

"What is it, Helen? Can you show me?"

I put the dildo slowly up to my mouth, watching her as I did so. Her eyes were suddenly wide open.

"Oh Helen, it's a giant cock."

I put out my tongue and started licking it, then I put the end into my mouth and as I did so, I lowered myself towards her mouth. I took it from my mouth and placed it next to hers.

"Lick if for me, darling."

Still looking amazed, Mary did not hesitate, quickly pushing out her tongue to touch it. I slowly rotated it and then gently pushed it between her lips. Almost in a trance, Mary opened her mouth and moved it forward, over the end of the dildo. I rocked it slowly backwards and forwards in her mouth, then I put her hand on it and asked her to hold it for me for a moment while I removed her knickers. Mary lifted herself so that I could more easily slide them off.

Then I took the dildo back and she watched, fascinated, as I buckled up the band around my waist.

"Helen? Will this feel like a real cock?"

I squeezed some lubricant into her vagina hidden amidst a jungle of curly hair. Then I placed the dildo against her and moved it slowly in, watching as I did so the magic of her vagina opening up to receive me. It was a beautiful sight.

"Is that okay, Mary? It's not uncomfortable in any way? Say if it is and I will stop immediately."

Mary's eyes were closed and her mouth was wide open. I heard a moaning sound, then suddenly Mary thrust herself up towards me and screamed "Yes, yes, oh Helen, yes!"

Mary had a new special friend, and I had a new lady-love.

I gave Mary a slow but serious shagging with the dildo and we both loved it. I would sometimes stop, but then the lower part of her body would thrust upwards and she would call out "More please Helen, more!"

Now I was ready. I wrapped a hand around each of her ankles, just above her bright blue high heels and lifted up her legs, speaking as I did so.

"Mary?"

"Yes, Helen?"

"Just so that you know. Having your beautiful stockinged legs and your shoes waving in the air in front of me fulfils a fantasy for me that cannot be beaten. If you ever feel that I'm not showing you enough attention, Mary, just say, 'I want my legs in the air please' and I will be your sex slave in seconds."

Mary giggled.

"Oh Helen. Everything about you is so beautiful. You shouldn't have told me that. I'll be texting you every day with that message. I will exhaust you."

We both laughed, then Mary went into a serious panting and groaning mode as I set about finishing off her first strap-on shagging, and with an orgasm that made her cry with happiness.

When we had finished and it was time for Mary to return home, she threw her arms about me and declared her love for me. Then as she was about to leave, she asked:

"Where can I get one of those, Helen? Just in case something was ever to happen to you."

We laughed and I promised to take her on a special shopping spree soon.

"There is another world out there Mary, and it is waiting for you."

Mary had said how because she couldn't make our usual tryst, her niece, Sophie had asked if she could spend some time with me instead. I was a bit shocked but Mary said that the young woman was excited at the idea.

I was a little on edge as I walked to my studio. I really hadn't had time to get to know Sophie. I knew she was a very capable farm girl with no boyfriend, and that there were very few young people her age in the region. I also knew that she had a certain look which I liked, and that underneath her trouser pants I suspected she had a nice pair of legs.

I tapped on the studio door to let her know I was there, and went in.

Sophie stood tall on a pair of high heels that she had gone shopping for with Mary the day before. Her stockings were a delightful smoky grey and she wore a shortish but conservative pleated skirt and a blouse buttoned to a frilly lace collar. Her face still wore that naive expression that I noticed when first we met, but there was something else going on suggesting a not-so-innocent state of mind.

"Hello Sophie, and welcome."

Before I could say another word, Sophie crossed the room and threw her arms around me and fastened her mouth on mine. I slipped my arms around her and pushed back on her lips; then her mouth opened and she put out her tongue and explored my now open mouth. We stood like that for a few minutes, then I slid my hand down her back and lightly felt her backside.

We eventually separated our mouths and Sophie smiled.

"Auntie said it would be best if I kissed you straight away, then I wouldn't be so nervous."

I laughed and turned her towards the bed, and we sat down.

"Dearest Mary! Did her advice work, Sophie? You're no longer nervous, I hope?"

"Yes, Helen, I feel relaxed with you now. Do you like my shoes?"

"Good! Yes, I love your shoes. I do have a bit of a shoe and foot fetish. Now Sophie, can I please do something, so that I won't feel nervous?"

Sophie looked at me with eyes shining.

"Anything!" she whispered.

I slowly unbuttoned my blouse right the way down and pulled it open, then I took Sophie's hand and drew it over my bosom and rubbed her fingers lightly on my bare breast.

"Please find a nipple, Sophie, and lick it."

Her face was a picture of surprise, delight and then lust. She put up her other hand and moved her face to my breasts, and within moments was nipping and tugging me with both hands and her teeth.

"Oh, you darling girl. You've made me feel less nervous already," I whispered soothingly.

Sophie moved back and stared into my eyes.

"That's good, Helen. Can I keep playing with you breasts, or would you like me to do something else?"

"In a little while Sophie, you know that I will want to shag you. I'm about to take off your skirt, beautiful girl. I can't wait any longer."

Sophie whimpered and shook as she absorbed what I was saying.

Her long legs swung wide apart and she stretched out, then she pushed her legs out more and pointed and rotated her elegant feet and footwear.

Immediately, I pulled up the hem of her skirt and looked at her.

Sophie's legs were indeed long and beautiful. Her grey elasticised stockings clasped the top of her legs, and above her stockings I saw that she had left her knicker off, probably on Mary's advice, and I stared at the mass of small shiny black curls all around her vagina and up and over her *mons veneris*.

"You are beautiful, Sophie," I murmured, lifting my head and kissing her lips. And when I put my hand out and touched her, lightly running my fingers up her stockings and between her legs, she let out a girly squeal of delight.

"Oh yes, Helen, please touch me! Touch me! Oh yes, Helen! Do anything you like. Anything! Please!"

I reached around and unzipped her skirt, then dragged it roughly down over her legs. Then I dropped onto my knees, put a hand around each ankle and lifted her legs and dragged her closer to the edge of the bed. Then I buried my mouth into that mass of curls in search of her lips and her clitoris, and when I found her surprisingly large soft happy cherry thing, I sucked it and felt her shaking body and her crying, and knew that she was mine.

After a while, I sat up. Sophie stared at me and smiled, then her lips made puckering motions, wanting to be kissed, and her tongue disappeared into my mouth. Sophie would not let my head go, and we kissed and tongued until we both ran out of breath.

"Helen darling?"

"Yes, Sophie?"

'Take off your clothes for me, please Helen. I so want to see you.

"Yes, darling, I will, and I love it that you ask for the things you want."

As Sophie watched, I slipped my frock off over my head, leaving me in my suspenders and stockings, and shoes.

Sophie stared at me, appreciation showing on her face.

"My God, Helen, you are so beautiful."

"Thank you darling. I do love complements," I giggled.

I got up on the bed and straddled Sophie, and backed up to her face. Her hands grabbed me by the hips and in moments she was ravishing my pussy with her mouth. I shuddered and felt my vagina getting extremely wet.

Then I lay down on Sophie so that I could reach her pussy, and we quietly licked and sucked each other for a long time, sometimes having little orgasms along the way, and occasionally Sophie would squeal and shout my name or just a "Yes," or "More please."

Then I turned and went to her, and we put our arms around each other and kissed, and then kissed some more. And then we rested.

I asked Sophie to close her eyes, then I stretched my arm down, felt under the bed and retrieved the strap-on dildo. Then I held it close to her face and told her she could open her eyes and look at the present I had for her. She was at first shocked and then very impressed with it.

"I wish Adele could see this," Sophie laughed.

"Is Adele your girlfriend back home?" I ventured to ask.

"Was, sort of. She lives on a farm about half an hour's drive away. I used to take the ute and go and see her once a month when her folks were away at the big market. Adele never goes to town to the market. She's a big girl, fat I suppose you'd say, and not very good-looking and she can't stand people looking at her. She thinks the whole world is laughing at her."

"That is really sad, Sophie. Surely there is a man for her somewhere?"

"I reckon not. She's never gonna change. It is sad."

"You live a long way from everything too, don't you? You must both get very lonely. Have you ever thought of being lovers?"

Sophie rolled over and looked at me, then leant closer and kissed me.

"Almost, I suppose. I let her lick me a couple of times, a year or so ago, and I gave her pussy an occasional rub and she did the same to me. But we stopped doing it."

I was intrigued. This was an insight into the extremely lonely life of isolated Australian bush communities. These were young women who lived without access to other people, to anyone with whom they might find love.

"Oh, Sophie. I can't bear to think of someone like you living without love. Did the two of you ever talk about what you might do to change things?"

"Sadly, not. Adele has just given up on life. I guess if she lived in the city she'd probably be a drug addict. As it is, she's addicted to Kenny."

"Kenny? I thought you said there were no males around?"

Sophie laughed.

"Sorry Helen, Kenny is Adele's dog. A Golden Retriever. She spends all her time bathing it combing it and kissing it. She lets ..."

"She lets Kenny what?"

"She gets Kenny to do her."

"I'm sorry, sweetheart, I didn't get what you said?"

"Adele gets Kenny to shag her. She loves it. And Kenny doesn't seem to mind."

I turned and got up on my elbow.

"Sophie! You are not making sense, darling. People don't fuck their dogs. You're spinning me a yarn and I'm not happy with this story."

"Gee Helen. I am so sorry. What I'm telling you is true though. I've seen them do it. Adele invited me out to a little room behind the barn that she's decorated and it includes a low bed. I thought she was just going to show me her room, but it was more than that. I saw it all happen there. Then she wanted to share Kenny with me. That's when I stopped visiting her."

I was not handling this information very well. Bizarre acts between people I could sort of handle, but sex with animals? That was too difficult.

"Sophie! I think this conversation is doing my head in. We better stop it. Tell me a happy story, please."

There was silence for quite a while. In the end, I thought I'd spoken a bit harshly to Sophie, so I moved closer to her and held her hand.

"Sorry, Sophie. I hate to think of you in such unloving circumstances. I just want you to be here with me and Mary, safe, and feeling loved.

"And I want you to tell me you will stay and live here next door to me. And one other thing, wrap that bloody strap-on around your waist and make love to me, please. And kiss me, Sophie. I want your lips right now."

Sophie took a sharp inward breath and moved swiftly, first with a long loving kiss, then she kissed my clit, and then she worked out how to put on the strap-on.

I directed her to the bottle of lubricant and she gingerly wiped some on me. Then she held and inspected her new piece of equipment, laughingly pointing out that she was a "dildo virgin", and hoped I would be gentle with her.

We both laughed and I pulled her head back down and kissed her again.

"I have loved the short time we've had together, Helen. Thought I should say that right now, just in case I get it all wrong and you throw me out in the next few minutes."

"Darling Sophie! All you need do is slide it in. What you do then does not much matter, just so long as you do it with love. Even if you get a little carried away, I will know that you still love me. Pop it in, darling."

Being shagged by my loving new novice was wonderful. I asked her to hold my legs up straight so that I could look at them and include them in my "legs to the sky" fantasy. She did that and said how super cool it was, and that she had never ever been this excited about anything. And then she kissed me behind the knees and touched my feet, and kissed and licked my thighs above my stocking tops.

She was a natural with the dildo, not too hot, not too cold, but just right. And I could see that she loved doing it to me. Sophie's face was alive and happy, reaching around my back to pull my buttocks up towards her. And when I came suddenly, she screamed and came with me, and suddenly Sophie was laughing and crying at the same time.

Then I unbuckled her and attached the magic rubber cock around my waist. Then I turned her over and made her get on her knees, lubricated her and whispered, "This is your reward for giving me such a wonderful shagging."

She screamed in a mixture of anticipation and fear, as I inserted it. I didn't really know what life experience's she'd had and I wondered if the dildo was too big. But it slid in easily and she straight-away settled down to a regular rhythm and was soon calling out words of endearment and encouragement as we went.

I rolled her over so that I could lift her legs up and satisfy my visual lust. She moaned as I lifted them and moaned again when I told her to open her eyes and see how beautiful she looked and how she had the most beautiful legs in the world.

"Oh Helen, I so love what you are doing to me. Please keep going."

I lay between Sophie's legs and shagged the beautiful girl some more, unable to stop myself. But when I slowed, thinking it might be time to stop, she announced in a clear but quiet voice that she would like "some more, please". And when I suddenly began to thrash about and pushing right up into her to test her limits, she screamed out "Yes, Helen, yes, Helen, please Helen, keep doing it to me, Helen!" before she screamed a final "Yes", and exploded in an almighty orgasm which echoed through her body, and mine, for the next five minutes.

We fell into each other's arms and I covered us with the quilt.

"Helen?"

"Yes, my darling?"

"I will definitely stay and live with Auntie. I'm in love with you."

We pulled each other close and kissed; then exhausted, we fell asleep.

When Helen called Mary and asked if she could visit her and Sophie on Friday night, Mary said that that would be wonderful and they would look forward to seeing her.

"Oh Helen, I've had such a week, you wouldn't believe. Sophie has been on top of me at least once every day with our new strap-on.

"She's a different farm animal each time she mounts me. A couple of hours ago she was a rooster. I hope you will be able to cope with her. She's gone crazy.

"Oh, here is Sophie now. It's Helen, darling. She wants to come over for the evening on Friday."

Helen heard Sophie's screams of delight and laughed.

"What is she saying, Mary? I can't quite hear her."

"She's beside herself with excitement. She says she's going to hide naked behind the front door, just wearing her new strap-on, and she's going to jump straight onto you."

"Gosh, I didn't know she liked me that much. Tell her, if it helps, Helen will take her panties off before she knocks on the door. Oh yes, one more thing, tell her not to forget the lube."

Mary laughed. She had switched on speaker phone so that Sophie could hear everything that Helen had said. Helen heard screams of excitement.

"Sophie says she is so excited and loves you 'muchly'."

True to her word, Helen slipped out of her panties as she knocked on Mary's door, planning to hold them up to the sexually frenetic Sophie as evidence of her willingness to let the country girl have her way. She was surprised when Mary opened the door wearing nothing but a robe.

"Helen? I'm waiting for you," came the voice of Sophie from somewhere in the house.

Helen looked at Mary quizzically.

"I should warn you, darling, Sophie seems fixated on farm animals. She's been on and off me all week and role-playing a different animal each time. Yesterday she had me as a billy goat and a rooster. As well as that, she's been back to the sex shop twice and she ordered a special something online as well. I will let you discover what it is.

"Oh, and my friend Janice is calling in shortly for our weekly coffee and cake session. I forgot she was coming and I couldn't get her on the phone to change the arrangement.

"Janice is my oldest friend. We were at school together. She is a singing teacher and helps the choir master at St John's where I sing on Sundays. I'll keep her in the kitchen."

Then a funny look appeared on Mary's face.

"It's odd really when you think about it. Janice has always had a thing for me and will often say that if she had been a man, she would have raced me off years ago.

"Well, Helen, I giggled to myself when I had a sudden thought today. I had the idea that I should hide a dildo under the kitchen table, then, just when Janice says 'If I was a man (etc)' I could pop it on the table in front of her and tell her 'Well here's your big chance Janice. I'm single now and I've got the hots for you too, dearie. How about it?'"

Mary was quiet for a moment.

"The thing about Janice is that, while she acts the innocent, I happen to know, from other sources, that she is far from it. Why she has kept her private life secret from me over all these years, I'll never know. Perhaps she thought I was so proper she couldn't divulge her deeper secrets. Who knows?

"I've always been secretly in love with Janice's skinny body and long legs. Opposites attract apparently, don't they? Now that you have pointed me in this new direction, Helen, I'm keen to get my hands on every skinny bit of her."

The two women laughed out loud. As they were about to walk off, Mary to the kitchen and Helen to the lounge, Helen said, "I think that is a great idea, Mary. But just remember though, they say be sure you really want what you think about, because once you've had the idea, it usually comes true."

Then Mary stopped and stood and looked at Helen and spoke. "Just to keep you up to date, Helen. Sophie applied for a job a couple of days ago and today they called to say she had got the position, meaning she is definitely going to stay here with us. Isn't that great?"

"Yes, that is good news. What sort of job did she get, Mary?"

"She will be a nurse's assistant with a veterinarian working with the racing industry. It turns out that our Sophie had a couple of very good references from her time working on stud farms. She will be able to study and move up to being a nurse if she wants to.

"She's very excited. She is now in a full-on horsy phase. When you find her in a minute or two, don't be too shocked.

"Her latest fantasy is that she is a mare about to be served and she has been restrained so that she won't kick and damage the expensive stud stallion. You will be the Arab stallion, and also the stud mistress who soothes the mare to ensure the mating happens.

"Welcome to Sophie's animal world, Helen. It's been a most entertaining week."

"If I'd known, Mary, I would have worn my jodhpurs and riding jacket, and boots."

"Now you are getting me excited, Helen. I think I could really enjoy a girl dressed like that."

Mary went off to the kitchen to make afternoon tea for her visitor and Helen headed for the lounge.

Helen's first thoughts when she saw Sophie lying naked across two footstools pushed together was how incredibly beautiful she was. Her strong body somehow reflected both her youthful naivety and her farm girl worldliness. In her manner, she seemed so self-sufficient and alive, and without any pretensions.

"At last, Helen darling! We can get started now, I hope," Sophie called.

"You are champion Arab stud stallion Sir Richard Burton, and I am Princess Fatima. He and I are of pure Arab stock and highly excitable, and your job as stud mistress, Miss Hot Pussy, is to get Fatima to take the giant donga of Sir Richard. This could be quite a challenge, Helen.

"And I hope you like the new strap-on. Found it online. It arrived this morning."

Helen saw that Sophie had wide leather imitation cuffs on her wrists and ankles, no doubt supposedly to stop her kicking and injuring the stallion, or moving away. What she also saw was the new strap-on. It was a huge replica of a stallion's penis, bigger than most of the dildos one saw at the sex shop.

Helen looked down at the beautiful Sophie. I think I can do this, she thought, smiling to herself, thinking back to the days at boarding school when the girls would go to the stables after class to groom the horses.

There wasn't a stallion at the school, but often the penises of the geldings would get quite big when they were being groomed, and some of the girls would giggle and make jokes and say things like "I hope I can find a boyfriend with one like that."

Helen could see the appeal and suddenly felt a tiny flutter between her legs. She picked up the heavy horse strap-on and inspected it. Instead of ending in a bulbous point like human dildos, this one was almost flat at the end, like a human one but sliced off. It was nearly twice as long and also thicker.

She removed her dress and attached the horsy thing around her waist and made sure it was firmly in place. Then she found the big bottle of lubricant.

"Ready, darling? I think Miss Hot Pussy is going to enjoy this."

"Ready, Helen!"

Helen added some lube to the end of the rubber donga and moved in to be closer to Princess Fatima. Then she attempted to add lube to the mare, but as she did so Princess Fatima whinnied loudly and moved herself to one side. She was having none of it.

"Easy girl. Take it easy, Princess. Everything is going to be fine. It won't hurt. Just relax."

Little snorts and heavy breathing came from the front of the mare.

Miss Hot Pussy touched Princess Fatima lightly with her fingers, all the while making soothing sounds. The mare responded, opening and shutting her vagina and trembling.

"You clever, beautiful girl. Just relax, Princess. You will like this once we get him inside you, I promise."

But when Sir Richard touched Princess with his penis, she threw her backside up and down and side to side and screamed a horsy scream.

Miss Hot Pussy stopped and reviewed the situation. Then she placed a hand on Princess Fatima's bare back and moved slowly forward along the mare's body, caressing her lightly and whispering nice things to her.

"There, there, Fatima. Relax and let me stroke you. Nothing bad is going to happen."

When the stud mistress got to Fatima's head, she touched her softly around the ears, then she put her mouth to an ear and licked inside it. Fatima gave a little horsy squeal and leant her head towards the stud mistress's face and tongue.

All the while, Miss Hot Pussy's hands were caressing Fatima. Then she ran a hand along the mare's flanks and under the mare, surprised to find, but happy to fondle, a delightful human-like breast. Fatima lifted her body enough so that Miss Hot Pussy could trace a circle around a nipple and stretch it and pull it downwards. Fatima made a not-so-horsy sound, a sort of gasp.

Then Miss Hot Pussy took a risk. She removed the dildo from around her waist and turned it on herself. As she did so she whispered nonsense things to the young mare, in a soothing voice.

The stud mistress was by now very wet, and after a few moments adding lube and spreading her vagina, she managed to insert the huge horse dildo.

Then she moved slowly around to the front of Princess Fatima, and got down on her knees and kissed her pouting lips. Then she licked a tear from Fatima's cheek.

"There, there, good girl. Easy, girl."

When the stud mistress stood up, she presented Fatima with her wet pussy with the giant dildo hanging from it.

"Good girl, Princess, don't be afraid."

Princess Fatima could suddenly smell the stud mistress's wet pussy. She made little whimpering sounds and put out her long horsy tongue and licked Miss Hot Pussy's pussy.

Then Princess Fatima moved her face down and began licking the stallion's penis, as Miss Hot Pussy moved it up and down slowly with her hand. All the while, Fatima gave little snorts and pulled back her lips, and gently nibbled at Sir Richard's penis.

"We like Sir Richard's penis really, don't we, Princess? Good girl," cooed Miss Hot Pussy.

"Now I think Sir Richard would like to offer it to your beautiful rear again. He will do so very slowly, Fatima. Just relax until he gets it inside you, just a little bit to start with. Then you will be in heaven, I promise. Good girl!"

The stud mistress slowly made her way back, kissing and caressing Fatima's body as she went, stopping to touch her beautiful breast again, and at her pussy to lick it and poke her tongue in and roll it around the mare's protruding clitoris.

Princess Fatima sighed and when Sir Richard's penis touched her, she opened up her vagina and sucked him in. Sir Richard kept up the forward movement until it could go no further, then he began a slow rhythmic movement.

When Princess Fatima orgasmed and screamed a horsy scream, Helen came too, much stronger than she had expected.

"Oh my God, Princess, what a darling little filly you are. Sir Richard and Miss Hot Pussy love you very much. Good girl!"

When Princess Fatima had orgasmed and she had hung limply over the cushioned stools for a while, Helen withdrew Sir Richard's penis.

As it left the beautiful Arab mare's pussy, it made a noise like a champagne cork popping, causing Sophie and Helen to burst out laughing.

"Oh Helen, that was amazing, so amazing. You are the most wonderful stud mistress in the whole world. Thank you from the bottom of my heart, oh, and other places too."

The two women laughed and hugged and kissed.

"Would you like to come to bed now, Helen? I would love to snuggle up with you and maybe have a snooze."

"Yes Sophie, I would love that."

———

At daybreak, Helen kissed Sophie goodbye and hopped out of bed and headed home through the gate in the fence.

She came into the house expecting the downstairs to be empty, and that she would enjoy a quiet coffee and read the Saturday newspaper she'd collected from the front garden on the way in.

She was surprised to find Freddy dressed in his silk dressing gown and already making coffee.

"There you are darling. I wondered when you'd be home."

Helen noticed how Freddy's smiling face was looking at her more eagerly than she would expect, given the time of day and, she assumed, after a possibly busy night with Alice and Freya.

"Yes, darling. I like to be at home on Saturday mornings, your day off, and looking forward to a weekend together."

Freddy switched off the coffee machine and came over to her. He put his arms around her and gently moved her backwards against the kitchen dresser. He kissed her lovingly and moved his hands up and down her back.

Helen enjoyed this moment, although she was still bringing her brain back from laying in bed with Sophie only minutes before. And her vagina was still wet from when Sophie, seemingly still asleep, rolled over in the early hours of the morning and touched and gently rubbed her pussy.

Helen realised that this was not a simple welcome home from Freddy, and when he turned her around and lifted up her skirt and touched her bottom gently and ran his fingers up and down the crack of her backside, she gasped. And when Freddy leant over to the butter dish and lifted the lid and pushed his finger into the butter, Helen knew where Freddy was heading.

Helen was lovingly enjoying Freddy's sudden obsession with her bottom. It had been ages since he had taken her in that way, and her excitement was palpable.

"Oh Freddy! I so love it when you're naughty in this way. Stay inside my bottom all day if you wish, darling. In fact I want you there all weekend."

"You are so beautiful, Helen. I'm crazy about you."

While this blissful domestic scene was in play, two sleepy girls arrived at the door of the kitchen from upstairs.

Alice and Freya stared at the buggering couple in disbelief. Freya reached out for Alice's hand.

Freddy was rhythmically reaming and disappearing into Helen's bottom while his wife repeatedly gasped, "Yes Freddy, yes Freddy, never stop doing this to me, Freddy, I love you my darling."

Freya took Alice's hand and wetted the index finger in her mouth then lifted her nightie and guided the finger into her bottom hole and wriggled and rolled her tiny bum about. Then she put a hand between Alice's legs and palmed her very wet pussy.

Suddenly Freddie called out to Helen.

"Sweetheart! I want to come."

"Yes, Freddy. Yes! Come in my bottom, you beautiful man."

Then the girls heard that sound again, the beginning of the growling roar they had each heard twice that night, as Freddy had taken each of them in turn.

Helen screamed as Freddy exploded inside. She slumped onto the dresser, sobbing.

"Oh Freddy, I love you so much."

The two girls tippy-toed back upstairs and threw themselves on to the bed.

"That is definitely something that is going on my list of things to do," whispered Alice. "Except Helen hasn't yet given me the anal sex lesson she promised me."

Freya looked at Alice and feigned jealousy.

"It's nice that she has offered to help you. I guess I will just have learn to do it all by myself."

Alice laughed.

"Darling, just ask her. She doesn't realise that folk like you and me don't know how, because she's been a devotee of bottom play for a long time and assumes everybody is the same as her."

"Of course, we'd have to work out how to get Freddy to do it to us first."

"You are right, Freya. And Helen just might not be keen to tell us how. She might want to keep that special thing with Freddy just for herself."

The two girls laughed and rolled about and, in their excitement, took turns lying on each other's backs and pretending they were Freddy, shagging each other's bottoms and yelling out, "Sweetheart! I want to come!"

Rosa had told Helen that it was best to get into Bertie's bed just after seven o'clock. By then he had gone for a pee, washed his face and brushed his teeth and then climbed back into bed and resumed an almost dreamlike state. Shortly after that, his erection would start to appear, and by seven thirty at the latest Morning Glory would be at the ready and happy to entertain a loving visitor.

Helen was understandably nervous as she found the hidden key under a flowerpot and opened the door of the Bennetts' house. Alice was not in the kitchen, as the two had agreed the day before that she would have her breakfast in her flat, and keep out of Helen's way.

Helen calmed herself and walked down to Bertie's bedroom. She knocked on the door.

"Come in, Alice."

Helen pushed the door open slowly and walked in, closing the door behind her. Bertie was amazed.

"Helen, sweet Helen, what brings you here so early in the morning? Is everything all right? Is Rosa all right?"

"Hello, Bertie. Yes, Rosa is just fine. She sends her love in fact, and, Bertie, she has sent me too."

"Sent you Helen? What do you mean girl?"

"Rosa and I are now lovers, Bertie, and she wants to share me with you, if you know what I mean. And if you are not comfortable with that, Bertie I can leave immediately, or though a cup of tea before I go would be nice."

Helen wasn't trying to be flippant. She was simply trying to avoid any long and overly serious discussion about the morality or appropriateness of what she was suggesting to Bertie.

Bertie stared at her, still in disbelief. Then he motioned to her to come over and sit on the bed beside him.

"Lovely to see you, Helen. I think about you a lot. We don't see enough of each other. I see more of your husband, which is not a bad thing. I love him dearly. He has a good head on his shoulders."

Helen sat on the bed beside Bertie, trying not to let him notice that she was looking for a lump in the bedclothes. Now that she was here she had a moment of self-doubt, of wondering if this had all been a mistake and that she shouldn't have come. Then Bertie made things clearer.

"If I am to share you, Helen, is there something you have in mind that we could do together? If not, I'd like to make a suggestion."

Helen realised that this was about to get serious.

"I would love to hear your suggestion, Bertie. I believe you already know that I have had a bit of a crush on you since I was a teenager.

"Rosa and I made a breakthrough this week, when she told me about her and my mother. During the conversation, she said she had always known how I felt about you and she thought you probably had similar feelings about me."

Bertie sat quietly for a moment. Then he leant forward and took her hand and slipped it under the bead spread and wrapped her fingers around his growing cock.

"Oh Bertie!"

"This would be a place to start, Helen. Rosa, when she is here, has it most mornings. She calls it her Morning Glory. Would you like to try what Rosa likes? We can think of other things we could do, later."

Helen's mind was racing. Yes, it did seem that Bertie's brain was working a little differently from most people's. And yes, Morning Glory was exactly where she wanted to begin.

"Yes, Bertie. I would like to try Morning Glory. Please tell me what to do."

"Before I do, Helen, I would like you to take off all of your clothes. I have wanted to see you naked for many years and it seems that at last, the moment has arrived. Please stand up for a moment and strip for me."

Helen needed no further prompting. In moments, she slipped off her blouse and bra and unzipped and stepped from her skirt. Then she pulled down her panties and dropped them on the floor and slipped off her shoes. She now stood before him in nothing but her grey stockings.

"That will do, Helen. How beautiful you are. Now I know why in times past, I have ached for you. Please come here so that I may kiss you and touch your breasts."

Helen went and knelt on the bed close to Bertie, and while she at first self-consciously tried to hide her body just a little, Bertie drew her close and began to lick her breasts. Then he drew her face close to his and kissed her on the lips.

"Are you ready, Helen?"

"Yes, Bertie."

Just as Alice had explained, Bertie told her to roll back the covers. And when Helen had done that, she reached out and took Bertie's big cock in both hands. Then she put it in her mouth. At last, after all these years she was the beneficiary of a mouthful of what she once craved. And then, when he asked her to swing around so that her rear was exposed to him, she shuddered just a little, knowing what was about to happen, half wishing she did not know what came next so that it could all be a surprise.

But while Helen was enjoying everything that Morning Glory provided, she also was enjoying Bertie for other reasons, one being that she was at last satisfying her desire to be this man's mature sexual partner. In the back of her mind also, were her expectations of adventures with Bertie using Rosa's codes, while sometimes sharing him with her beloved Alice.

When Helen – at what she thought was the end of this delicious adventure – found herself being held by Bertie's hands, tightly clasping her hips, she sensed there was a change of plan.

Bertie rose from the bed and dragged Helen around so that she was kneeling with her rear close to the edge of the bed and close to Bertie's cock.

"Helen. Don't be frightened if I get a little carried away. I don't usually ejaculate, but on this special occasion, I want to celebrate having you, so if you are OK with this, I will give you a very good shagging and come inside you. Can I go ahead, Helen?"

Helen thought quickly, but just as quickly knew she wanted it.

"Yes, Bertie. I'm very happy that you want to do this with me. Please shag me as hard as you want, lovely man."

Like Alice before her, the earth did move for Helen. But not only that. When things subsided and she went and brought the cups of tea and they had finished them, Bertie informed her that he had enjoyed her so much that he was now wanted to shag her again.

Helen lay panting, totally blissed out on Bertie's second magnificent ejaculation, and as sperm dribbled in huge quantities from her stretched and pummelled vagina, Bertie told her that he hoped to see a lot more of her and that he thought Rosa would be very happy to know how well they had got on.

But then it was Helen's turn to have her moment with the man she'd had a crush on all those years.

"Lie back down on the bed, Bertie. I haven't finished with you, my darling."

Helen settled herself on top of Bertie with her back end close to his face. Then she mauled his testicles and his cock, sucking him and licking him and even biting him and rubbing him between her breasts, doing everything she could to make up for those years of wanting him, and in her mind she saw herself with him in her teens, her twenties, her thirties and on and on, until today.

Helen wanted to fulfil and satisfy all those years, and she wanted Bertie to know how she felt. And when Bertie gently licked her, and caressed her buttocks and her shoulders, and lifted both her feet to his mouth and sucked her toes and licked her ankles, she sobbed and she knew that he understood.

"Yes, Bertie. You will see a lot more of me. And yes, I'm sure Rosa will be very happy. Thank you, you lovely man."

It was the day after Helen's first erotic encounter with Bertie, and she was feeling very pleased with herself. She had phoned Alice and put her on notice that they should think about what they could or would do on their first 'Fifi' code session with Bertie. Helen had a few ideas which passed dreamily through her head as she settled in her studio.

Helen looked at the painting she was working on. Leaving a work for a couple of days was always a good idea. To look at it with fresh eyes allowed one to see faults and things that could be improved. As she was looking, for some reason she remembered something Mary had said about Janice, something which suddenly fired her thought processes and she remembered something important.

Only a couple of weeks ago, Helen had been at an art gallery opening, and sitting with a group of women, some of whom she had never met. She got on well with a pleasant lady who talked about interesting things, not just the usual boring holiday plans or their forthcoming sea cruise.

Helen could not remember what led to this particular conversation, but this woman's story went something like this.

The woman, Celia Ashbee, had a son teaching at a private school whose friend, teaching at another private school, had a friend who told him a rude story. The friend of the friend of the friend said that one of his senior students and some other lads were in a church choir and that they had a great time each week after choir practice with two women.

Helen suddenly got very interested at this point, but tried to hide her enthusiasm, not wanting the nice lady to think ill of her.

"Did the friend of the friend of the friend say if the student described what happened, Celia?"

Celia poured more tea and selected a savoury *petit four*. Helen estimated that she was perhaps a little older than herself, a well-kept woman in her late fifties or very early sixties.

Celia continued her story, lowering her voice and looking around her as she spoke.

"It seems that the music teacher and the organist would wait until everyone had left at the end of practice, except for a half dozen or more lads who went and hung around in the churchyard.

"Then the two women would go back inside the vestry, change their clothes, putting on stockings and suspenders, high heels and short skirts, along with lots of makeup, then unlock the door and let the boys in."

Helen found the story fascinating, and erotic.

"My goodness, Celia, stories like this could cause a sudden increase in the sizes of congregations across the land. Please tell me more."

Celia laughed, enjoying her new friend's sense of humour and impressed with Helen's seeming lack of shockability.

"Did he say what actually happened after the boys entered the vestry?"

Helen's new friend coloured up and Helen looked at her appreciatively. Celia, on the one hand a very proper upper middle-class woman of impeccable taste, hid a fun-loving naughty side which one would never have observed except via the subject matter of this conversation.

"He did, Helen. He did indeed. He said that in a very small ante-room there was a mattress covered with a bedspread, probably an emergency bed in case someone in the congregation suddenly took poorly.

"He said that the two women knelt on the mattress and called to the boys to come in, in pairs. Then they told the boys to show them what they had in their trousers. Once they were on display, each woman would put a boys penis in her mouth and suck it; then after a while they would look up at the boy's face and say ..."

By this time, Helen was mesmerised by Celia's story and, it should be said, by the delightful Celia. Her looks, her beautiful voice, her smile, even the lines on her face spoke of intelligence and joy. Her fine clothes spoke of finer garments beneath, a satin camisole perhaps, expensive serviceable panties with just a touch of lace? And was she a woman who preferred wearing stockings or did she choose tights? And even though she was slim, would she own a corselet?

"Say it, Celia. Tell me what she said. You are committing story interruptus. Please, don't leave me hanging."

Celia burst out laughing, then put her hand over her mouth and looked around like a naughty girl.

"Suck or fuck?" she whispered.

Helen stared at Celia's sparkling eyes, bright with mirth.

"Gosh Celia, we're getting to the high notes now."

"Then, if the boy replied with the 'f' word, the woman immediately does an about face, showing her rear end and, it is said, not wearing any knickers, at which point the boy has his way.

"If he has any difficulty finding his way, and if the woman beside her is facing the front and has a moment with a free hand, she will lean across and put him in. If not, a hand will come through the legs to grab him and sort him out."

Celia stopped talking and stared at Helen. She looked flushed and excited. She was fascinated with Helen. She loved her relaxed unfazed way of seeing things.

Helen looked back at her, one could even say lovingly.

There was suddenly a hush as people prepared for a final concert piece by three young violinists.

"Celia?"

"Yes, Helen?"

"Can I write down my telephone number and give it to you? And maybe we could catch up some time soon. I love talking to you, so I hope we can see each other again."

"Please, yes. And I will call you very soon. You are great company and I do get lonely for someone to talk with who is happy to talk about anything."

"Thank you. Oh, I forgot to ask, can you tell me the name of the church or do you need to keep it a secret?"

"Ah, yes. I hadn't really thought about that. Perhaps if I just say it begins with a J, Helen."

"Hello, Helen."

Helen had walked over to the house to get a knife sharpener. She always meant to buy one for the studio but then, when shopping, she forgot.

Helen was startled by the voice. She looked up.

"Sorry Helen, if I surprised you. I came through Mary's gate and saw you leaving and that you had left the door open, so thought you would no doubt return soon."

"Janice! How nice to see you. Are you looking for Mary? I think it's her volunteer day at the Salvos' op shop."

"Sort of. But I really wanted to see you, Helen. Can I come in?"

Helen gestured towards the studio door.

"Be my guest, Janice."

Helen could not move her eyes away from the long, thin extraordinary body of Janice. Her legs and backside were almost a kinky artwork, exaggerated in a way that artists toyed with in their drawings but which quite rightly, no one ever believed depicted a real person.

But what was racing through Helen's mind at this moment was what she had said to Mary, "Be careful what you think about because it usually comes true." She had thought quite a bit about Janice since her conversation with Celia Ashbee about the goings-on at the church, and Helen was convinced that, 'J' must surely have meant St John's, and if it did, then Janice was surely one of the women entertaining the boys after choir practice.

And hadn't Mary said she thought Janice was not as innocent as she looked?

Helen steeled herself. Other than her fascination with Janice's body, she felt no special attraction to the woman. She had no thoughts about loving her and without any emotional ties it would be hard to imagine that anything would ever happen between them.

Helen closed the door and invited Janice to sit on one of the studio's three kitchen chairs.

"Well, Janice. What can I do for you? Is Mary giving you a hard time?"

Janice laughed.

"Not at all, Helen. I'm not sure how to say this, but I was always fascinated with Mary's story of your seduction of her, and how beautiful and loving it was. Over time, I've not exactly been jealous, but Mary took me quite brutally, not showing any love until later. Now whenever I think of love, I can't help thinking of you, Helen. Could we be lovers too, Helen? It would be a wonderful thing, sharing you with Mary."

Helen's mind raced as she watched an increasingly agitated Janice first lift her skirt up just above her knees and then fiddle with the buttons on her blouse, while her mouth began to gape and her tongue wandered over her lips.

Helen could thank her for her compliments and then simply ask Janice to leave. There was no way she wanted to add Janice to her list of girlfriends. And then of course there was the deceit of the woman, if she was one of the women in the story about the lads at St John's. Her story about wanting to be loved did not in any way ring true.

Helen suddenly saw what was going on. Janice was under an influence of sorts. Was it drugs? Helen guessed it was something she had first heard about many years before, when she was working in a clinic in London.

Janice was suffering from what, in the old days, was called nymphomaniac's disorder, known amongst Helen's co-workers and nurses as nympho block.

The word "nymphomaniac" was no longer in use, having been replaced with the term "hyper-sexuality", but in those days, the term "nympho block", referred to a woman who had engaged in sex continuously over many days, weeks or months, and who was now unable to live without it, suffering a craving like a drug addict looking for the next fix.

Of the various theories that doctors and therapists came up with, the one Helen found most plausible was the idea that these women had experienced a lot of bad sex or, put differently, incomplete sex, sex without orgasms.

Normally, regular sex between partners might be very satisfying, or it might not. The difference was that women who only had sex a couple of times a week, and did not experience regular orgasms, did not suffer this build-up, or if they did it was minor and could be overcome. Sadly, what was more likely to happen was that they just learnt to live with it or should one say, without it.

One solution offered by sex therapists was to teach a patient to orgasm more easily when having sex, and in the couple of cases Helen observed this did, over time, lead to a better outcome for the woman. And of course, the arrival of the electric vibrator changed things for many women.

What Helen was seeing here might well be the result of Janice having a lot of inexperienced young cocks giving her nothing but their quick ejaculations. These lads were not experienced males offering foreplay and long deep thrusting and prolonged enjoyment.

Unable to find a fix, Janice had finally ended up here as a last resort. Subconsciously, she understood the need for real love and, remembering Mary's story of her loving conversion by Helen, this was the only place where she might find answers.

Helen looked at Janice and saw that she now had her hand between her legs, her head had lolled back, and her eyes were closed.

Then she recalled an experience she'd had in London. It was her first real lesbian romance. The older woman was Louise Lazarus, the glamorous bitch secretary of the medical centre's managing director.

Helen was dazzled by Louise's stylish clothes and elegant body, and when she invited Helen to her flat for afternoon tea, one Saturday, Helen jumped at the invitation. After she had arrived and been shown around the luxury apartment, it was only an hour or less before Louise had her tongue inside Helen's mouth and a hand inside her brassiere, and it wasn't long before she was guiding the young woman's hand along Louise's stockinged leg and up to her panties, where she lovingly showed the willing novice how to put her fingers inside her crotch and inside her.

Louise had secrets that she carried from her schooldays, and over time she revealed those secrets to Helen.

Louise had been educated at one of the smaller private girls schools near the Sussex border, in Kent. The school, or rather the staff, were expected to follow the school's long traditions regarding discipline, meaning that girls were regularly thrashed.

Flagellation or "pursuing the path of penance" as it was referred to, was a regular occurrence at the school. So endemic was it that "the art" was practiced, not only by the staff on the senior girls, but the senior girls themselves who would administer it to a select few of the staff, always in secret of course.

Whippings, strappings, spankings, floggings of every description were a major topic of conversation. Everything at school rotated around who had what done to them, or what they had done to someone else.

So popular was this pastime that it would seem to have been the foremost form of entertainment for the hormonally charged scholars, and quite naturally girlfriends looked after one another, tending each other's discomfort with soothing balms and very loving words.

Thus "pursuing the path of penance" facilitated the continuation of the school's healthy lesbian traditions, endowing the nation with the strong women necessary for providing the special sort of workers and wives required to serve alongside the public school men of the aristocracy and the upper classes, and ultimately to ensure the success and safety of the empire.

Stately homes, along with the nice houses of the public servants taking the early morning trains to Westminster or the City in their bowler hats – and with extreme punctuality – were ruled by women of substance, women who knew where their responsibilities lay, along with their understanding of certain things that their husbands didn't know that they knew.

Adaptability was an essential quality for the public school educated woman, especially when she eventually took her marital vows, and shouldered the responsibilities that being a wife demanded, be they judging the flowers at the village fete or organising the house staff on an Indian tea plantation, or overseeing the affairs of the family and the estate, while her officer husband was away on some foreign battlefield.

Within days Louise had made Helen her protege, and shortly after that her sex slave, having Helen whenever, however and wherever she wanted.

From then on, Helen felt a wetness between her legs whenever Louise spoke her name, and she bent her knees just a little the moment her mistress came towards her.

The medical centre where Helen and Louise worked specialised in gynaecological problems. Woman would present with all sorts of situations, and every once in a while, if there was someone with a case of hyper-sexuality who was suffering, the powers that be would give a wink and nod, and indicate to Louise that this might be a case of "nympho block" and that she could perhaps help the sufferer.

Helen remembers returning home to Louise's house one evening after working late. Immediately she shut the front door behind her, she heard screams which she knew could only mean that someone was being flogged.

Knowing better than to disturb her mistress in full flagellator mode, Helen nonetheless, went and listened at the door of the punishment room.

Things had obviously been going on for some time. The person being flogged was well past screaming "No, please, no more" and now sang out in a high pitched wailing scream, "More, yes, yes, oh please, more." This was followed a little later by a deafening scream that seemed to go on for ages, as the woman reached her orgasm.

As Helen turned to leave, the door flew open and Louise walked out and seeing her, and with her eyes shining brightly from the excitement that she had just enjoyed, grabbed her and kissed her passionately on the lips and, pushing her against the wall and with a hand firmly placed between her legs, said "I'm going to give you an orgasm like that, darling, very soon," then headed to the bathroom.

And she did. Only days later, Louise took Helen into the room and closed the door and proceeded to introduce her to the strap. She already new that the pain would turn to pleasure, but when it did became pleasurable, Louise didn't stop. Only when Helen vented the prolonged scream which accompanied a major orgasm did her lady lover stop beating her, and instead, took her in her arms and carried her the few steps to the big bed. But she hadn't finished.

First she lightly rubbed balm on Helen's cut up bottom. Then she put on her favourite strap-on and opened her legs and shagged her, all the time telling her how beautiful she was how sexy she was and how she was going to fuck her forever and a day.

Once a week, after work, Louise would tell Helen to put on her old school skirt and the long school socks she had saved, hidden in a drawer. Then she would make her lie back on the bed while she lifted her legs, staring at her while she ran her hand up her schoolgirl sock to the bare top of her leg, all the while touching herself with her other hand.

Then Louise would give her her evening shag. And when she had given her an orgasm, she would look down at her with her beautiful smile and say "You've been such a good girl all week Helen, Miss Lazarus is going to let you have her pussy now as a reward. You can shag her just as much as you want, my child."

Then she would lift Helen up and take off her strap-on and fix it to her waist.

As Helen worked the dildo in and out of Louise's splendid pussy, and as Louise lifted up Helen's skirt and touched her legs, she stared up at her young and innocent face and spoke softly to her. "Do you love shagging your teacher, darling? Does being on top of Miss Lazarus excite you my sweet? Yes, I know it does because you are shagging Miss Lazarus so beautifully." And so Helen's introduction to love also included other people's fantasies, and she loved them.

Helen's first lady lover became her yardstick for any future relationships and she chose mostly to be a single person rather than enter into what she always sensed would be a liaison less intense than the experience the dazzling Louise had shown her.

Janice was staring at Helen with pleading eyes.

Helen looked up at objects hanging on the wall. Among the interesting miscellany of items was a well-made leather tickler, a miniature cat-o-nine-tails that Freddy had brought home as a present for her when he had been away at a convention.

She was excited when one day he picked it off the wall and laid into her bottom with it. She screamed in agony, but just as she was beginning to get a wonderful sensation that overrode the pain and would take her "all the way", Freddy stopped, believing he should not hurt his wife in this way. Helen was extremely disappointed. "That is what comes from having such a caring husband, damn it!"

The little tickler had not been taken off the wall since.

Helen was now getting hot thinking about that day with Freddy, and much further back to Louise, and the possibilities in front of her now. She could help Janice and enjoy herself at the same time.

Janice's amazing legs could not be ignored, Helen mused as she stood up and went over to her.

"Janice?"

"Yes Helen?"

"I'm going to do things to you. Okay?"

"Oh yes, please Helen. Please give me some relief. If you don't, I think I will surely die. Do whatever you want to me, Helen. It must be better than dying."

"Janice?"

"Yes?"

"I'm going to whip your backside, Janice, until it turns red, and I won't let you leave until I'm finished. Are you ready for this, Janice?"

"Yes, Helen. I need to be punished for I have sinned heavily in the sight of God."

Helen knew enough about addicts. They loved to be theatrical and talk rubbish, though often it did relate to some real event in their lives.

"Would you like me to kiss you first, Janice, before I thrash you?"

"Yes, yes, give me your lips, Helen. I so want to be loved."

At first, she wanted to kiss Janice only to make it easier for her to launch herself on the wretched woman. Now Helen was going to love her properly, regardless. She could whip Janice with love, just as Louise had whipped Helen.

Helen led her to the divan beside the window

She began by kissing Janice, who cried and thrust her tongue into Helen's mouth. Helen accepted it, tentatively at first but then, deciding to let herself go all the way. She put her lips back on Janice's mouth and tongued her enthusiastically, while Janice groaned.

Then she slipped Janice's skirt down over the long legs and made her lie down on her back. Helen lifted her legs high up in the air as she did with all of her lovers, and told her not to move.

Helen grabbed a charcoal pencil and a pad and quickly sketched the magic legs and the unusual bubble backside, incongruous on such a thin body.

Then Helen slowly caressed Janice's legs and kissed the backs of her knees, and all the while Helen couldn't stop touching her own wet pussy and she smiled inwardly, knowing that this was a good sign.

Janice continued sobbing, all the time murmuring, "Yes Helen, yes Helen, please Helen." Then Helen reached for the tickler on the wall.

When Janice screamed the giant scream that accompanied her most extraordinary orgasm ever, Helen orgasmed too, and not just lightly. The excitement she felt while flogging Janice's rear end felt as though Janice was the one who had flogged Helen. It felt truly beautiful.

Suddenly two women, who until now, had been separated by many differences, were sharing feelings that were very rarely available to women other than via a flogging, be it by hand, the rod, or the tickler.

Janice was cured, at least until the next time. Her manner changed and Helen hoped that her habits would change. But that of course, would be up to Janice.

Helen never knew just what happened at the church after that, nor did she bother to ask. Nor did she enquire about what other things her new sexually hyperactive friend got up to.

But she knew that this new secret friend, Janice, would come to her with her long legs and body each time she felt a "nympho block" coming on, and together they would visit that secret heaven.

Helen bathed Janice's backside and delicately applied a healing balm. Janice lay still and quiet as though she was sleeping, but when Helen said in a very quiet and reassuring voice that Janice could come to her whenever she needed special help, she turned her head and with a serene smile murmured "Thank you, Helen."

And when Helen went on to ask Janice if she would keep their special time together a secret, Janice replied, "Only you and me, Helen, I promise." Then she looked up again and added, "and our little leather friend, hanging up there on the wall."

Helen put a hand on Janice's face and kissed her. "Just the three of us, darling, that's right."

Then Helen rolled Janice onto her back and lifted her legs so that they stood high in the air.

"Now Janice, please don't move for a moment. I just want to add the seams of your stockings to my drawing."

Helen found Celia Ashbee's house. It was very large and set in an acre of trees and shrubs with lawns around the edge of the sweeping drive-way. Large iron gates swung closed behind her as she drove in.

She had texted Celia when she was on her way so that the gates would be open when she arrived.

Everything seemed so grandiose, even more so when she was greeted at the door by a pretty maid who showed her through to the parlour.

"Miss Ashbee will be with you shortly, Mrs Alves. Please make yourself comfortable."

Helen thanked the maid, thinking what a beautiful young woman she was.

Once alone, Helen wandered around looking at pictures on the walls and photographs on the cabinet tops.

She was particularly taken by a number of black-and-white photos showing the young Celia in various activities: with other players holding hockey sticks; riding a beautiful horse in what looked like a dressage event; Celia throwing a javelin at an athletic meeting. A picture Helen liked above all others was Celia standing with two girl friends, all three in bathing costumes.

"Sorry to keep you waiting, darling. Phone calls can be such a nuisance. Come and sit down and we'll start with a cup of tea."

Celia went to a corner near the huge fireplace and pulled on a thick silk chord. Almost instantly, the maid appeared.

"Polly, this is my friend Helen Alves. We would like tea for two. Oh yes, and could you bring a couple of meringues too. Thank you, Polly."

The two women had a pleasant conversation about all sorts of things, laughing a lot at shared jokes and stories.

Then Celia invited Helen to follow her to show her a little bit of the house, but in particular her favourite room.

The study was delightful, lots of books and antiques, and quite lavishly furnished with two enormous sofas and two very large armchairs as well as an ottoman and various footstools.

Celia shut the door and the two made themselves comfortable on one of the sofas.

From the very beginning, when first they met, Helen had been fascinated with Celia's wonderful voice and deportment. And the more time she spent with her, the more she admired Celia's trim body; and she adored her face.

The two had just stopped laughing about something, when Celia leant forward towards Helen and smiled.

"I think it's time I kissed you Helen. I hope you will be neither offended or frightened. Come closer, darling."

Helen was mesmerised. She had lived through many seductions and knew what to expect; or not. Celia's offer came not so much as a surprise, but because Helen fully expected that the initiative would most likely have had to come from her.

Helen instantly appreciated the offer.

"At this moment, I can think of nothing I would want more than to be kissed by you Celia. You are an enchantress. I'm feeling a little vulnerable at this moment though, so please be gentle."

Celia smiled appreciatively and Helen moved up closer to her.

"I will tell you what I would like us to do, if that is fine with you Helen?"

"Yes, Celia."

"I have fantasies, Helen. Seductions are a common one, and teasing is another, not that I get to experience them often. Would you accompany me on my fantasy, beautiful woman?"

"Yes, Celia. I have fantasies too, so I can appreciate your need more than you can know. Please Celia, have your way with me in your fantasy, in any way you want me."

"The rules are that you must keep your eyes closed and you must not move. My fantasy is teasing you."

Helen was excited. She felt a tiny moment of excitement in her pussy and a sudden dampness between her legs.

"Please begin, Celia. I am waiting dear, lady, and you are making me wet already."

Celia smiled in appreciation of Helen's comment. Then Celia made sure Helen's hands were properly placed beside her thighs and that her eyes were closed.

Helen surrendered to Celia. All she wanted was to be a part of Celia's fantasy, wherever it took them.

After what seemed a long time, Helen felt the lightest touch on her breasts, but then the touch was gone. Then she felt fingers lightly touching her on her stockinged knee, but then they were gone. A moment later, a gentle rubbing on each ankle made her want to respond and stretch out her legs and feet, but she knew she must not move.

Then, moments later, fingers moved slowly up the backs of her legs along the calves, stopping to pirouette behind her knees before moving further up and under her skirt.

Then Helen felt her skirt being slowly lifted as Celia revealed the tops of her legs. Fingers touched her suspenders, then lightly touched the wet spot on her panties. Helen could not contain a trembling, but managed to stop the tiny orgasm that would normally follow it.

A silent, motionless period followed. Then Helen felt Celia unbuttoning her blouse and when she had undone all of the buttons it fell open, revealing her braless top and her beautiful breasts.

Fingertips touched the tips of Helen's hard stiff nipples.

Helen heard a little gasp from Celia, then realised that she, herself, was breathing heavily.

Then Celia spoke, and when she did, Helen realised that she had heard that voice, long, long ago. Louise Lazarus, her first love, her lesbian mistress and the woman who had converted Helen to a love of discipline. Could Celia Ashbee be another ex-private girls-school student like Louise?

"Now little girl, if you are ready? Open your eyes and unbutton Miss Ashbee's blouse, just as she has unbuttoned yours. That's a good girl. Don't be scared."

Helen was both shocked and delighted. Never ever had she expected to find a soulmate in a fantasy that she held dear to her heart. Helen had no difficulty in reverting back to Miss Lazarus's schoolmistress and schoolgirl fantasy. She had adored Louise playing the schoolmistress.

Helen opened her eyes and smiled at the beautiful Celia. Helen leant forward and began to unbutton Celia's blouse.

"Yes, Miss Ashbee."

Helen noticed a moment of surprise on Celia's face.

"What a good little girl you are, Helen. I might have to think of a special treat for you later."

Helen had undone the buttons and was staring at the lace bra covering Celia's elegant chest.

"Now girl, before we take Miss Ashbee's brassiere off, she would like you to try and put your little hand down inside the garment, and find the nipple on her left breast. Off you go, child. See what you can do."

Oh, what a delight this woman was. Helen figured that she could play this game all day and still some. She was definitely warming to being the little Miss Helen.

Helen's hand touched the top of Miss Ashbee's chest, then she slid it down behind the left bra cup and captured the beautiful nipple, already standing to attention. She fingered it lovingly.

"Oh yes, you beautiful girl, you are making your teacher very happy. Oh yes!"

Then Celia leant forward and, reaching round, unhooked her bra. She slipped off her top and slid the bra shoulder straps off, then she dropped it on the floor.

She lay back for a moment, her shapely breasts staring at Helen, and Helen staring back, running her wet tongue around her lips in anticipation.

"Would you like to kiss Miss Ashbee's breasts, young lady? And would you like to sit on Miss Ashbee's knee little girl, so that you can cuddle up to her bare chest?"

"Oh yes, Miss Ashbee. Please let me. I'm feeling quite queer, but it is a lovely feeling. I think it's because of the things you are doing to me Miss Ashbee. Please don't stop."

"Before we do anything, sweet girl, Miss Ashbee is going to take off her skirt so that she can better enjoy you sitting on her legs. Would you like Miss Ashbee to take some clothes off?"

"Oh yes, I would love that, Miss."

"And I think we should take some of your clothes off too, darling. While I remove my skirt, you take off your top and skirt. Then come and sit on my knee."

"Oh yes, Miss!"

Helen quickly removed her clothes and stood in front of her fantasy school mistress in her panties, stockings and heels.

Celia stared at her, feeding on the beautiful vision. Then she took Helen's hand and sat her on Miss Ashbee's now exposed stockinged thigh.

Celia couldn't stop herself. She groped Helen between her legs and cupped her breasts and eagerly slurped and sucked her very stiff nipples. When she stopped, she leant back and smiled.

"You sweet girl. You are so beautiful, I might never let you go back into class again. I might make you my slave and keep you in my quarters. I would come and make love to you many times every day and teach you how to love and be loved. Would you like that darling little Helen?"

"Oh yes, Miss Ashbee. Please! I would love that. And Miss Ashbee?"

"Yes, darling?"

"Please let me kiss your lips. I love you so much."

"Oh, what a joy you are. Come to me, you sexy little wench. Put your tongue in my mouth while I think about which part of you I want to have next."

With that, Celia rolled back and to the side to lie on the sofa, dragging Helen with her, pulling her face to hers and kissing her passionately while touching and fingering little Helen between her legs. When they eventually stopped, Celia whispered in Helen's ear.

"Darling Helen. Where would you like our fantasy to go? Do you have a thing that you want desperately enough that you would beg Miss Ashbee to do it to you?

It didn't take long for Helen to respond.

"The truth is, Miss Ashbee, I adore discipline. Spanking in particular. But apart from a relationship I was in, in London during my early twenties, I've never found anyone that shared this same urge. I know much about how to "pursue the path of penance", but it is not something others know about or wish to share."

Helen realised that Celia was crying.

"What is wrong, Celia?"

Celia sobbed.

"Nothing, sweet Helen. You have just made me the happiest person in the world. I too had given up on ever experiencing the delight of proper discipline. So often my bottom has longed for a strong loving hand.

Now we can explore each other in that way. I am so happy. Thank you so much."

Helen lay on top of Celia, gently rubbing herself against her. Then she had an idea, and spoke in her pretend schoolgirl voice.

"Miss Ashbee?"

"Yes little Helen?"

"Earlier you said you might find me a special treat."

"Yes child, I did. Did you have something in mind?"

"Yes Miss Ashbee, I do."

"Well, out with it girl. What special thing would you like Miss Ashbee to do to you?"

"It's something that I would like to do to you, Miss Ashbee. I would love it if you let me give you a spanking right now, and later I would like you to spank me, Miss. The older girls talk about it a lot and say they get a lovely feeling between their legs after the first painful moments. And they say you are the best mistress to do it. They all say they love you for it. Please, Miss Ashbee? Let me do it to you. Please?"

Only moments later, Celia answered Helen's call.

"I would love you to spank me, young lady. You can have my bottom and do whatever you want right now and I shall have yours later. How could I not want to feel your hand on me?

"Let us move to that ottoman over there. You will sit and I will bend over your knees and we will spank our way to heaven."

And they did.

Helen and Celia did a lot of kissing after they had enjoyed a marathon of mutual spanking. They laughed and lusted, cried and cringed, screamed and creamed, and all the time made love to each other every which way.

When they had worn themselves out, they still wanted to be together. With their arms around each other's waists the two wandered back into the lounge and Celia called Polly to bring them refreshments.

Polly brought in a tray. She really was a beauty and Helen looked at her with searching eyes, but couldn't help noticing an air of disapproval when they made eye contact.

"Celia? I believe that Polly doesn't approve of me. She gave me a very black look when she came in. I wonder what I've done to upset her?"

Celia smiled.

"I noticed that, darling. I think the young lady is suffering a painful dose of jealousy. I wouldn't mind betting Polly had her ear to the study door earlier, and heard us screaming. I'll sort it out with her later."

"So can I take it that she could be in love with you, Celia?"

Celia blushed slightly, and coughed.

"Let's say she is just discovering life, shall we Helen?" She looked at Helen coyly.

"Ah! So you have practised your seduction techniques dearest Celia?" I responded severely, "And I thought I was the first in recent times."

Celia kept blushing but laughed loudly.

"You might not believe me when I say it was an accident."

Helen laughed, "Pray, please do tell."

"I had initiated the earlier maid, Jacki, into the delights of love over a period of a month, but she was so highly energised by the whole experience that one day she ran out and dragged the young gardener – who worked here two days a week – into the greenhouse and had him on a pile of weed matting, then immediately fell pregnant.

"Fortunately for all concerned, me included I suppose, young Brad was so impressed with Jacki's sexual know-how that he proposed and they are now happily married.

"Jacki made Brad leave my employ, afraid of what might happen if and when the next maid – her replacement – found her handsome man in the garden.

"I should just mention here that, when Brad called in to tell me he was leaving, I thought I couldn't just let him go without giving him something to remember me by.

"I was alone in the house, as I hadn't yet found a maid.

"I got Brad to follow me into the library and sat him on the sofa. I told him how much I had admired him and the work he did, and would he do just one last thing for me?

"Nervous and in a hurry to please me, and I suspect a little besotted with me, he said I could ask him for anything.

"I sat close beside him and took his hand and said that, as I was unlikely to see him ever again, would he do me the honour of pleasuring me with his manhood.

"Then I pulled up my skirt and dragged his hand onto the top of my leg and then I reached across and unzipped him.

"In moments, I had his rapidly expanding cock in my hand, and moments later I dragged off my panties and dress and brassiere while he took off all of his clothes.

"Then he laughed and impaled me on his cock and ran around the room clasping my buttocks in his hands, and lifting me up and down on his cock, while my legs rocked backwards and forwards like I was riding a hack in a cross country event.

"It was a lovely moment, Helen, as I'm sure you can appreciate."

Celia paused and reached across and slid her hand backwards and forwards over Helen's knee.

"Well, you amazing woman. What a wonderful send off-for him, one he will never forget I'm sure."

Helen put her hand on Celia's and guided her to the back of her knee and made her stroke the back of her thigh.

"The truth is, Helen, Brad now pops in every couple of months and I give him what he calls his finishing up present. I do so like a cock occasionally, Helen, it's important for ones health."

Helen laughed as she stretched her leg.

"I suppose I should really call it 'a bit on the side' Helen."

Helen threw her arms around Celia and they kissed passionately. Celia slid her hand further up Helen's skirt and caressed the tops of her legs, snapping her suspenders.

"Oh Helen, you are so wonderful. I'm so wet and it's all your fault."

"I'm falling in love with you more every moment, Celia. And the reason you're so damned wet is the same reason I am, because of your super randy stories, you sexy bitch.

"Now, let's get back to the seduction of Polly, Celia."

"Following the incident with Jacki, I deemed it better to control myself and not allow myself to seduce any staff.

"I do have an older Italian woman come in to prepare authentic pasta meals for the freezer, once a month. Fortunately it's on the last Thursday of the month, which is one of Polly's days off.

"Aurora comes from strong Italian peasant stock and laughingly throws me around the kitchen as if she was a man.

"We have our zucchini time just before she leaves to go home to cook her husband's dinner.

"Aurora's body has some remarkable features that I am sure you would appreciate. Her lower front is covered with a thick mat of curls. It's as though she had a beard, going from her inner thighs up to her navel. Not only that, she has the biggest clitoris I have ever seen, and yes darling, I've seen a few.

"And I believe that, before she comes to work, she fills her knickers with sweet smelling herbs, rosemary and thyme. I can usually get an idea of her moods from her aroma. If she is very quiet and I cannot smell herbs, I say very little. If she smells beautiful and is singing her Italian opera, I know she will be more than happy to play our games.

"On her singing days, I greet Aurora with a big wet kiss. Then she lets me drag down her big knickers and bury my head in her mass of sweet-smelling pubic hair while I search out and mouth her magic clit. It's her very own little penis. And when she comes, I hang on to that superb object with my lips, and my head shakes."

Helen was agog as she slowly unbuttoned Celia's blouse.

"How wonderful, Celia. What happens next?"

"Well, after that, dear woman, I let Aurora have me however and wherever she wants.

"I moved a day bed into a corner of the kitchen, just for us, but Aurora loves to hoist me up on the central kitchen bench and, in her words, eat me out. Then she enjoys doing me with a large zucchini while I lie on top of her on the bed, sucking her giant nipples and almost suffocating in her cleavage.

"Interestingly, Aurora says that after a zucchini day at my place, her husband picks up her hot vibrations the minute he gets home.

"Serge is a concreter, shorter than Aurora and as broad as he is tall.

I only met him once when he came to collect her one day. He must be the original ball of muscle.

"The way Aurora tells it is that Serge showers as soon as he gets home. Then he comes and finds her, usually in the kitchen, where he first sniffs her around the neck, then lifts her skirt and inhales between her legs, then he takes her from behind. When he does that, she knows she's in for a busy evening, with him in her for most of the night, every which way, including her backside."

Celia stopped and laughed, and moved her fingers further into Helen's panties.

"Aurora always thanks me, and laughingly says that Serge only started doing this after we started having our zucchini time.

"I would love you to come and enjoy zucchini time with us. Aurora is extremely well built and has such a lovely personality, and she is very appreciative of any lewd attention. She would just love to get into you, I'm sure."

Helen stared at Celia with new eyes. This woman knew what she wanted and how to get it.

"So I guess we should get back to Polly. How did this accidental seduction come about, Celia? Tell me! I so want to know."

"Well, I needed a book from the study and went to get it.

"Unbeknown to me, young Polly had been dusting there and had discovered the cache of adult toys that I keep in a zipped bag inside the ottoman. She didn't hear me come through the door. Polly was sitting back on the sofa with her skirt up and her knickers down around her knees, rubbing herself while enthusiastically sucking on a dildo.

"I watched, enchanted, as you can imagine, but I couldn't contain my excitement and went to her. She was mortified when she saw me and screamed. But I spoke gently, telling her that what she was doing was quite natural, and that all intelligent women and girls did it.

"She was speechless and couldn't stop staring at me. So I slowly lifted my skirt and slid my hand into my panties, and rubbed myself a little. Polly stared with even wider eyes.

"Then I sat down beside her, picking up the rapidly discarded dildo from the floor, then slowly lowered my panties to around my knees to mimic the way she was sitting. I placed the dildo in my mouth as she had. Then I said to her, 'Polly, let me show you how Miss Ashbee uses this thing.'

"Then I slid the dildo into me then, ever so slowly, began to work it. Then I closed my eyes, hoping that Polly would not choose the opportunity to run away. I played with the dildo for a while and when I opened my eyes and looked at her, Polly's eyes were closed and her mouth hung open and she was busy touching herself between her legs.

"She opened her eyes and looked at me and I smiled reassuringly and Polly, looking a little pale and wan, smiled weakly back at me.

"I decided to move on, hoping not to frighten her. I reached across and picked up her spare hand and rested it on my pubic mound, moving her fingers around a little. She jumped a tiny bit but didn't take her hand away, looking at it with bright eyes.

"Then I put my spare hand on Polly's fluffy little mound and moved my hand around a little bit, then put two fingers on her clitoris. Polly gasped. Then I leant over and kissed her on the lips and almost instantly she kissed me back. Emboldened, I offered her my tongue, slipping it slowly between her lips, and moments later she touched my tongue with hers.

"I wasn't sure what I should do next, she was so beautiful and I didn't want to frighten her. But then I reached up and undid the buttons on her top and put my hand in, and slipped two fingers into her little bra and wiggled a very stiff nipple.

"Polly cried out, but stayed where she was. Then I unbuttoned and opened my blouse and reached back and unfastened my bra, and pulled Polly's head down to my breast. Polly gasped again, then pushed her mouth over a nipple and gently licked and sucked me.

"Then I whispered in her ear that I was about to come, and not to be frightened.

"She took her head from my breast and stared down at the moving dildo. Then she gingerly reached out and touched it, then put her fingers around it, clasping it and moving her hand up and down with me as I pushed in harder.

"When I came, I screamed and the darling girl screamed too, staring at my contorted face. Then she grabbed my hair with her free hand and pulled it over, and kissed me passionately. Then she slid her tongue over my bare breasts.

"Then Polly screamed loudly and her body shook as she orgasmed and I grabbed her and held her close to me, and after a little while I whispered, 'Did you like that Polly? Would you like us to do it again one day?'

"Polly put her mouth up to my ear and whispered, 'Oh yes Miss Ashbee, I did love it and yes, I would love to do that again'."

"That was around a month ago, Helen. She and I have come a long way since then. Polly is wonderful and I love her dearly, but I realise now that she has become a tiny bit possessive, so I should do something about that.

"Her petulance might give me a good excuse to introduce her to a little discipline.

"Now you and I have become lovers, I will gently lead her to the idea of us sharing ourselves with you."

Celia and Helen kissed a long beautiful farewell kiss and said their goodbyes, agreeing once again that they had been very lucky to have discovered one another.

Celia's parting words sounded enticing.

"I'm pretty sure that when you visit next time, you will have two people waiting with their lips puckered up looking for your lips Helen. And who knows, you might find more than just one person willing to show you their derrière.

"Sweet dreams darling."

Wednesday with Alice was going to be exciting this week, thought Helen, as she drove into the Bennetts' driveway, thinking about their forthcoming adventure with Bertie and the codes.

Alice smiled lovingly and kissed her at the door. She was feeling exhausted from her hectic exam week at university and explained this to Helen saying that she was not feeling very loveable.

Helen laughed out loud.

"What could your lover possibly do right at this minute that would help you take your mind off this? I'll do anything."

Alice kept her unhappy look on, then, taking advantage of Helen's sympathy, and like a spoilt child, demanded to know when she was going to get her anal sex lesson.

Helen laughed, thinking this was incredible. Then, in the most matter-of-fact voice she could muster, she replied.

"Right now, actually. Will I remove your knickers, or will you do it yourself?"

It was Alice's turn to look stupefied.

"You aren't serious, are you?"

Helen got up and walked over to the sex toy box.

"Never more serious, my darling. I am going to enjoy myself having your beautiful backside for my very own today. If you lighten up, I might even make it work so that you can enjoy it, too."

Alice's face was changing. She was suddenly eager and willing to enter into the spirit of the game.

"All right, wicked stepmother. I will allow you access to my posterior on one condition."

"And what will that condition be, my darling?"

"You have to immediately come to me and take off my bra and kiss my breasts, spread my legs wide apart and lick my pussy, then roll me over and have your way with me with that pink thingy you're holding in your hand."

The next few minutes saw the two screaming at each other while grappling with their clothing and body parts.

Alice tore Helen's top off and bit her nipple so hard she shrieked in pain. Helen lay on top of Alice and pretended to shag her very hard. And finally, they threw their arms around each other and hugged and kissed and rolled around the bed, passionately devouring whatever body part they could get their mouths on.

Finally, Helen rolled Alice over on her tummy.

"Pink thingy time, darling. Hope you like it."

"Oh no!"

Alice lay quite still as Helen squeezed some lubricant into her bottom. Then she closed her eyes and screwed up her face as she felt Helen's index finger in her; then the pink thingy slid effortlessly into her smooth bottom passageway.

"There, darling! So far so good, would you say?"

"Yes Helen. Now what?"

"Now, sweet girl, we play mummies and daddies, or if you prefer, just girlfriends. But I'm the daddy one. So look out mummy."

Helen began a slow in and out with the pink thingy and Alice lay still, reflecting on what was going on.

Then Helen increased the speed a little and Alice began to get a feeling she hadn't known before. It was all so slippery and soft, but also so very nice. Helen thrust the pink thingy in and out, and as she did so, she put the fingers from her other hand on Alice's pussy and gently played with her clitoris.

Alice relaxed her backside, and began to move it around in time with Helen's bottom play. Then, as she felt her clitoris yearning for more of Helen's attention and as she visualised images of Freya and Helen's beautiful legs in the air, Alice orgasmed, and as she did so she felt an exquisite echo of it in her backside.

"Oh yes, Helen. That was beautiful. A two-in-one happy ending. I love you, Helen, and I'm going to love anal sex. Thank you, you wicked stepmother."

"You can seduce me with your bottom anytime, darling. I'm on call twenty four hours a day."

Alice rolled over and grabbed her and showed her appreciation with her lips.

As Alice made tea and toast for the two of them, Helen reviewed the code list and called out to Alice and asked if she had made her list.

Today was the day they were going to decide which codes they would use when they shared Bertie later in the week.

Bertie was out on a coach trip learning about drought management techniques on farms. Saving water was one of Bertie's big interests.

As they finished their late-morning tea and toast, Alice suddenly suggested that, with Bertie away, they could nip down and see the picture of Fifi fixed to the inside of his wardrobe door. Given that Fifi was the motivating key word in all of Rosa's codes, this seemed quite a good idea. They too would then have an image of her when they went to Bertie and requested his services.

Alice and Helen felt like naughty children as they stole into Bertie's bedroom. They had, of course, both been in there before, but for just one purpose: Morning Glory.

Alice opened the wardrobe and the two crowded in to meet Fifi.

There she was, the classic, alluring, sexy French maid, guaranteed to excite the carnal lusts of any man, and many women too.

The Fifi postcard was not alone. A postcard depicting a large pair of smiling, bright red lipsticked lips was stuck to the door, along with another card showing just a pair of feet wearing high-heeled fashion sandals.

Helen laughed.

"We'd better pile on the lipstick darling, and make sure we've got the right shoes. We want Bertie to have his fantasies satisfied too."

Turning to leave, the two faced the bed. Both stopped, unable to leave the bedroom without remembering what they usually came in there for. Then Alice looked at Helen. In a flash, the two were rolling on the bed, each holding a handful of wet pussy and yelling: "Morning Glory! Morning Glory! Thank you, Bertie."

Alice and Helen sat on the sofa in Alice's flat, drawing up their Bertie Menu, as they called it.

Alice was back on form, energised no doubt from Helen's attention, both to her front and to her backside.

"We mustn't be too greedy or demanding, I suppose? Do you think we can have more than three things? Can we have seconds? Are side dishes counted as one? If there are two of us, does that mean three codes would equal six as we are sharing? We mustn't exhaust him!"

"If it's between Bertie and us, from what I've seen of him I'd bet that we'd be exhausted before Bertie was."

"Oh, darling Helen, I so look forward to that exhaustion, specially as we will be doing it together."

The two laughed and compared notes, and eventually agreed on their list and also which Fifi code they would ask for first.

Then they did a last-minute check of the sunroom and set a day and time for their Bertie adventure.

Helen made a note to buy another lipstick and Alice thought it was a good time to shop for new shoes. They were both extremely excited and when they kissed each other goodbye they agreed that the planned adventure was going to be exactly that, a real adventure.

Alice and Helen had picked a day when Bertie played bowls in the morning, then came home and showered, and spent the rest of the day in his greenhouse or garden shed. Alice had a pretty good idea of the time they should approach him, but they decided, just to be sure, they would make certain to be in the kitchen a half hour beforehand.

The two dressed themselves in Alice's flat. During a phone call a couple of days earlier, Helen had said that she was thinking of wearing a black corselet she had bought earlier in the year, but had never worn. Alice liked the idea so much that when she was out shoe shopping she lashed out and bought a black corselet too.

The two women had a lot of fun dressing for their Bertie adventure, all the time deliberately avoiding the temptation to touch each other in their lascivious enthusiasm.

"We must save ourselves for Bertie, Helen."

"Can't I unbutton your corselet just the once Alice? Please?"

Applying their makeup felt like dressing for a pantomime. Face powder, mascara, eyeshadow and lipstick.

"Perhaps Bertie would like us as geishas?" Alice suggested.

"He might. He served in the Far East and might have been in Japan on leave. Must ask him one day."

Alice pranced around the bedroom wearing her new shoes, getting used to them and worrying that she might not be able to walk far. Helen looked at her and burst out laughing.

"Darling! You only have to waddle from the kitchen to the sunroom. After that you'll be either on your bum, your knees or your back," to which Alice replied,

"I just don't want you beating me to it, wicked stepmother."

The two went over to the house and mucked about in the kitchen enjoying a constant banter, things like who looked the most like a tart, or how they would be received if they went to the mall dressed like this.

Suddenly, they heard Bertie coming along the passageway. Both women experienced a short pang of excitement and a sort of panic, but when he saw them, kissed each one on the cheek and commented on their beauty, they knew that it was game on.

"Seeing you two together dressed up like this is really exciting. Where are you both off to? The races perhaps?"

"No, Mr Bennett. We thought we'd play dress-ups and then hopefully, hang out with you for a while as we see so little of you. Helen agreed to come over to help me enjoy the end-of-term holiday. We were just thinking of moving into the sunroom and would love you to join us."

Bertie looked at the two women, inspecting them from head to toe.

"I would be mad to refuse such an offer. Lead the way, Alice."

Helen and Alice each put an arm through one of Bertie's and led him through to the sunroom.

"Is there a game or activity that either of you had in mind?"

Helen and Alice looked at each other. This was the moment when Alice would ask the question.

"Well yes, Mr Bennett, there is. Mr Bennett, Fifi and her friend would like to suck your cock."

There, it was done. What would happen now? The two women looked at Bertie's face. Were they conscious that they were wearing an exaggerated adoring eyes look?

Bertie looked at each of them in turn then clasping each of the women's elbows in his large hands, he led them to the sofa and turned and looked at them.

"Now, Helen, and you too, Alice, it will be truly delicious for me and I will enjoy our time much more if you were both to take off your dresses so that I can see more of you. I would like to see your breasts. Please do that now."

The two women looked at each other, then reached down and raised their dresses above their heads and took them off. Bertie stared at the two beauties in their corselets and stockings and shoes.

"You are both very beautiful."

Then Bertie leant forward, first to Helen, loosening her corselet so that the part covering her breasts fell forward and exposed her nipples. Then he did the same to Alice.

Then he undid his belt and dropped his trousers and underpants around his ankles and, as the two women stared, lifted his heavy penis out from between his legs, holding it up as he sat down on the sofa.

"Now, kneel down on the carpet, the two of you."

The two women went down on their knees in front of him.

"Sweet Helen. Would you like to start?"

Alice watched, fascinated, as Helen moved her head forward, taking Bertie's huge cock in her hand. Then Bertie reached a hand forward, grasping Helen gently by the hair and dragging her head and those bright red lips to his cock. Helen opened her mouth wide and engulfed Bertie's manhood and began to slowly move her head up and down.

"Alice dear, you could touch my testicles and help Helen when she needs it. I'll leave it all up to you. Thank you. Oh, and I must tell you that you both have beautiful breasts."

Alice ran her fingers around Bertie's testicles while she looked at Helen and at her stiff nipples.

After a little while, Helen turned her head towards Alice and removed the cock from her mouth and offered it to her. Alice took it and straightaway began to suck it. Helen's hands were suddenly free and she reached over and fondled Alice's nipples.

Alice flashed her smiling eyes away from Bertie long enough to acknowledge her appreciation of what Helen was doing.

"You are both amazingly beautiful women. I love you both dearly and I love what you are doing."

After what seemed a considerable amount of time, Helen signalled Alice that she was happy to move on.

"Bertie, Fifi and her friend would like you to have them over the back of the sofa please," Alice said softly.

Bertie smiled and stood up, lifting the two women by their arms as he did so. Then he led them around to the back and one at a time bent them over at the waist and placed them over the back of the sofa and pulled down their panties. Then he spent a little time, inspecting and touching them and making sure his entry to their vaginas was not impeded by their corselets or suspenders.

Alice and Helen, hanging over the sofa back, were free to exchange adoring and delighted looks, and exchange kisses, and touch each other breasts.

"You first this time Alice."

Bertie took hold of his member and rubbed it up and down against Alice's vagina to wet it before inserting it. Alice gasped and closed her eyes while Helen held her hand tight against her bosom.

Then Bertie started to shag Alice, gently at first but then harder, until he reached his preferred rhythm.

Alice looked at Helen and smiled, then whispered.

"Darling, I think I'm going to orgasm shortly. Just letting you know."

Helen squeezed her hand, acknowledging her message, then purposefully took one of Alice's nipples and clutched it tightly, so that she could better feel Alice's explosion.

After Alice screamed and convulsed her body and yelled 'yes Bertie', he stopped his thrusting, but remained in her for some minutes, allowing her to have a second and third tremor.

Helen had also experienced a small orgasm as she held Alice's breast.

Then Bertie slid his cock out of Alice and straight into Helen. He moved it slowly around and around, as if he was searching for something, or maybe wanting to stretch her vagina, but the effect on her was significant. Helen fully appreciated his "looking around inside me" action before beginning to shag her.

When the girls resumed their mutual touching and kissing while Bertie did his job on Helen, Helen whispered that she would come quite soon too, and Alice moved a hand to hold one of Helen's nipples, as Helen had done with her.

Helen didn't scream but she did a lot of noisy groaning, climaxing with three very loud explosive grunts, while Alice experienced ongoing trembling, resulting partly from her earlier orgasm but triggered by Helen's deep release.

Again, Bertie chose to stay put inside Helen until he was sure she had been properly fulfilled. Then he withdrew.

"Thank you, Bertie. That was truly beautiful."

"For me too. Thanks. I do love both of you."

After a few moments, and furtive looks and smiles at Helen, Alice plucked up the courage to make one more request.

"Mr Bennett?"

"Yes, Alice?"

"Fifi and her friend would like to have you on your back."

Bertie laughed.

"I could probably do with a bit of a lie down."

Then he walked around to the front of the sofa and lay down, his massive cock waving happily at the ceiling.

"Who's first?"

Alice and Helen stood up straight and stretched, and looked at each other and laughed. Everything was certainly going to plan.

Having Bertie on his back would give them an opportunity to ride him and be totally in control. They had earlier speculated whether they would be able to experience yet another significant orgasm. Also, having Bertie this way would be a lot like having Morning Glory, and they wanted to know whether it would feel the same.

Alice went first, clasping his cock, then climbing on him and sliding him in to her very wet vagina.

She was now in charge of their movement and the speed and impact of him against her body. What was different from Morning Glory was having her lover Helen with her, touching and kissing her.

Moving up and down on Bertie was a wonderful sensation and she could have happily done it for a lot longer, but there was a mission, and Alice dedicated herself to seeing if she could orgasm a second time.

Helen touched her with light finger caresses as she moved. Sometimes she would touch Alice's nipples as they bounced around in front of her, and with her other hand she palmed her own pussy. The two were indeed sharing every moment.

Alice came, again with a scream; not only that, but she remained sitting quietly on Bertie's cock, then felt the urge to repeat what she had done and very soon screamed and came again. Then she did it a third time.

Helen stared at Alice in amazement.

"I doubt I'll be able to do that, darling. You are amazing."

When Helen climbed onto Bertie and began her ride, she wasn't sure how things would work out. She'd had the super orgasm earlier. Did she deserve another? Even with her darling Alice's caresses, was it even possible?

Another lot of noisy groaning and climaxing with loud explosive grunts heralded the success of her efforts. She slipped off Bertie's cock and lay on top of him. He put his arms around her and kissed her, and Alice bent her head down and kissed each in turn.

Just when Alice and Helen thought that they had all finished, Bertie spoke.

"I would very much like to shag your beautiful mouths, dear ladies. If you would both sit up on the sofa, side by side, I will have you; very gently, I promise."

Helen and Alice looked at each other with raised eyebrows, then smiled.

"Are we side dishes or dessert, I wonder?" murmured Helen.

Bertie thought what a picture they made, sitting on the sofa, looking quite dishevelled but happy, legs slightly apart and their breasts sticking out above their half-opened corselets, and showing off their beautiful stockinged legs and suspenders, and their delightful feet and high heels. And he loved the way his two favourite women kept a hand between each other's legs. And here he was, with two bright red open mouths waiting to be fed with his big cock. It couldn't get better than this.

Bertie's cock moved in and out of Helen's heavily lipsticked lips and mouth, then he transferred it to slide in and out of Alice's mouth and then back to Helen again and then back to Alice.

The girls managed to get a quick smile at each other, and even a whispered message, in between their mouths hosting Bertie's member.

"I am so loving this," said Helen.

"Me too! I'm going to stock up on lipsticks."

"We should buy in bulk. I think we're going to use a lot."

"At this moment, I just want to be a Lippy Whore."

"Me too!"

"Helen! Do you know if there is going to be another book, a follow-up to this one?"

"There will almost certainly be one, Alice. Sorry, I forgot to tell you when I arrived. We just received word that Rosa is coming home from hospital next week, which means that things will change around here. There will be plenty to write about, Rosa will make sure of that."

Alice and Helen noticed that Bertie had stopped his gentle thrusting and looked up at him.

They all agreed to stop. Alice and Helen thanked him for a most enjoyable afternoon and Bertie thanked them both for their delightful company. Then he excused himself and headed off to tend to what he described as a "pressing orchid pollinating event" in his green-house.

"I think pollinating could be Bertie's middle name."

Alice laughed, enjoying the irony of Helen's remark.

"Oh yes! There is another thing I haven't told you, Alice. Number nineteen next door to us has been sold, and you will never guess who's bought it!"

"Who has bought it, Helen?"

"I mentioned it to Rosa in conversation when the billboard went up. And guess what? She made a phone call to a friend who bought it two days later. Want to have a guess who the friend was, or will I tell you?"

"How could I possibly guess? Tell me, Helen. Who is your new neighbour?"

"Maude!"

"Oh my God! I knew she was tired of all the travelling and wanted to move in from the country, but this is certainly a bit of a shock. Look out Helen and look out Freddy too. And wait till I tell Freya. We are already worried about all your hot action with your other neighbours."

"And that is not the only change happening in the street, Alice.

"Right next door to Maude in number 19, number 21 has a new owner. They've apparently inherited the property.

"Word has it that the new owners are a successful author currently living in London and his step-sister. Both will be moving back to Australia shortly. I don't know their names. I have been given to understand that they are both single.

"It is a huge old two-story house with a separate unit at the back, much like the one Bertie and Rosa have here. It is a beautiful property set in an established garden and on a double block. It will be interesting to see what they do with it. Exciting times Alice, don't you think?"

"Indeed, Helen. Eros Crescent might never be the same again."

Since Helen's first visit to her new friend Celia Ashbee, the two had not had an opportunity to meet again, though not for want of any lack of desire to renew their newly forged romantic alliance. Both women had reasons to travel away and their presence in Sydney seemed never to coincide because of their busy lives. Now the two women were finally getting to meet again, and again it would be at Celia's house.

It was the middle of February and the Australian summer was merciless in its heat and dryness. Helen had selected a bright floral summer frock and her favourite sandals for her visit. There was no place for heels and stockings in this weather.

Helen had already left home to make an early call on Rosa at the hospital before moving on to Celia's house. It was only after walking from the hospital that she got a message from Celia saying that she had been called away for a short time and would be a couple of hours late getting back to the house. She suggested that Helen delay her visit or, if she was already on her way, continue and perhaps enjoy the pool at Celia's house.

Helen thought about it and decided that it wasn't worth returning home and, as there was nothing else for her to do, she would head to Celia's place. The pool idea sounded great, although it had not occurred to her to bring her bathing togs. She reasoned that she might be able to borrow a pair from Celia.

As she knocked on the door, Helen was suddenly reminded of her last visit, particularly the moment when they were saying their farewells to each other. During Helen's visit Polly, the beautiful young maid, had acted in a very unfriendly manner towards Helen and when Helen mentioned it gently to Celia, Celia had replied: 'Poppy is wonderful and I love her dearly, but I realise now that she has become a tiny bit possessive, so I should do something about that.

Her petulance might give me a good excuse to introduce her to a little discipline. Now you and I have become lovers, I will gently lead her to the idea of us sharing ourselves with you. I'm pretty sure that when you visit next time, you will have two people waiting with their lips puckered up and yearning for you.'

Before Helen could finish thinking about this, the door opened and the beautiful Polly stood in front of her in a simple floral-halter neck dress and sandals.

"Hello Mrs Alves. So nice to see you again. Do please come in. You know that Mrs Ashbee will be a little late, but she hoped you would find something to occupy yourself with until she arrives."

Helen stepped forward out of the bright sunlight into the darkness of the vestibule and, as she did so, Polly wrapped her arms around her, put her mouth on hers and kissed her in a way much more than cursory but not long-lasting.

"Oh Polly, what a dear young woman you are. I so appreciated that kiss. It's the first I've had from a woman in many weeks."

Helen thought that lying in this instance would do more good than bad, giving the girl confidence that she was indeed special. As her eyes grew accustomed to the shadows, she thought that Polly seemed to be blushing, but she couldn't be sure that it wasn't just the hot weather.

"My word, it's cooler in here. Thank goodness for air conditioning."

Polly led Helen to the big lounge room. Helen immediately recalled her seduction by Celia and, later, their cavorting and mutual spanking on the foot stool near the piano.

"This is such a lovely room, Polly. And I have fond memories of it, as I'm sure you would too."

"Can I get you a cold drink, Mrs Alves? We have a lovely fresh lemon and ginger drink."

"That would be lovely, Polly. Oh and bring a glass for yourself. But before you go …"

Polly turned and took a quick step towards Helen, her eyes bright and questioning. "Yes, Mrs Alves?"

"Polly, I think you had better get used to calling me Helen when the two of us are alone together. "Mrs Alves" sounds a bit too formal for most situations. Is that all right with you?"

"Oh yes, Mrs Alves, I mean Helen. I would like that. And Helen, please feel free to relax and enjoy the place as you would if Mrs Ashbee were here."

Helen observed the excitement on Polly's face and concluded that Celia had indeed presented the idea of sharing her with the two of them, and sharing was now firmly impressed on the young maid. In fact, if Helen wasn't mistaken, young Polly was very keen to begin sharing.

When Polly returned with the drinks, Helen had already made herself comfortable on the large sofa. She had picked up and was thumbing through a magazine when Polly returned.

"Mrs Ashbee phoned again. She said she is dreadfully sorry, but she won't get home now until just after three o'clock. I said you were here and she suggested you might like to wait for her but she would understand if you left and made another time. It is around midday now, Helen."

"Hmm, not sure what to do, Polly. Stay or go and come back another time?"

"Well, if you stayed, Helen we – I mean you – could spend some time in the pool. I could make some lunch and you could just relax."

Helen watched Polly closely. She seemed a little agitated.

"And if you stayed, we could get to know each other better."

Polly's voice tailed off to a whisper and she definitely blushed. Helen was excited at seeing her trying not to show her enthusiasm for some sort of encounter. The dear girl was definitely "hormonally charged" as the magazines liked to label sexual urges.

"Well, you make staying sound good, Polly. And I can't think of nicer company than you. But I didn't bring bathers so, if it doesn't bother you, I will have to skinny dip or swim in my panties."

Polly's face reddened even more.

"Oh, that would be just fine, Helen. Nobody can see the pool area from outside the property."

"You will of course come in with me, won't you, Polly. It's not much fun on your own."

"Whatever you say Helen," replied the girl, nervously clearing her throat and reaching for a drink.

Helen reasoned that is was time to put Polly out of her misery or rather reduce the poor girls hormonal fuelled tension.

"Polly?"

"Yes, Helen?"

"Before we go to the pool, would you come and sit beside me and let me kiss you? Your lips were so soft on my mouth when you kissed me at the door, I haven't been able to get over it. Please, Polly. Come here and kiss me."

Polly stood up from her chair staring at Helen and, as if in a trance, stepped over to the sofa, where Helen took her hand and gently pulled her down beside her. Then Helen put her hand behind Polly's head and brought it up close to her face, all the while staring into Polly's beautiful grey eyes.

Helen wrapped her arms around Polly's upper body and drew her close while opening her mouth and pressing it against Polly's pretty lips. Polly let out a tiny groan and melted into Helen, opening her mouth and pushing out her tongue and slowly moving it around inside Helen's mouth. Helen pulled the girl even closer, and at the same time, nestled the two of them down into the soft sofa, where they stayed for a long time, kissing and touching and holding each other very close.

When Helen had filled herself up with kissing and cuddling, she announced softly that she wanted Polly to put her hand up her frock and take off her panties.

Polly murmured a little sound and pushed her soft lips even harder on Helen's mouth. Then she turned and looked down at Helen's knees and reached out to touch them and lifted the hem of her dress. Her fingers wandered up Helen's legs which opened just enough that Polly could touch Helen's sex behind the front of her wet panties. Helen lifted herself from the sofa and Polly drew the panties down over Helen's feet.

"Now finger my pussy, you darling girl while I touch your breasts and kiss your neck."

Polly was breathing deeply and she uttered sounds that told Helen the young woman was already in a rapturous state, as indeed she knew was happening to herself. Kissing and making love slowly was the progenitor of anticipation, and anticipation rivalled orgasm as the peak of sensuous feeling.

Helen bent Polly's head forward so that she could slip the neck strap over the girl's head and let her frock fall down around her waist, exposing her small breasts to her appreciative gaze and her softly groping fingertips. Polly shuddered when Helen lightly pinched the young woman's nipple, causing Helen to enjoy a tremor in her vulva, where Polly's fingers were massaging and entering the wet special place.

Helen was now on fire and crazily wanting more of this beautiful young woman. Helen's anticipation levels were so high, she couldn't bear the thought of letting go of Polly right at this moment. Then, as if from nowhere, Helen saw her late teenage self making love with her first real lover, Miss Louise Lazarus, and immediately knew what she wanted.

At that time her small hands had become a means of pleasuring Miss Lazarus in a special way; so much so that soon her lady lover could not long do without it. On a Sunday morning, the normally severe Louise would look at the young Helen with a soft dreamy smile and say, "Please give me your hand, my pet. I'll give you whatever you want afterwards." Now it was Helen's turn to enjoy that thing that Louise had taught her to do.

"Polly?"

"Yes, Helen?"

"Reach over and get the lubricant from that cupboard beside you, sweetheart. We are going to need it."

Polly tried to read what the purpose might be on Helen's face, but then turned and fetched a bottle from the side cupboard.

"Now I want you to cover your right hand with lubricant, Polly."

"Yes, Helen."

"Now put three fingers into me and move them around inside to stretch me a little."

Helen watched as Polly did what she was told.

"Now put your other fingers in as well, and push them right up into me."

Helen looked lovingly into Polly's face, feeling the sweet young thing's hand inside her.

"Don't be scared. Now slowly move your fingers up into me. Just move them gently and keep on going. And give me your mouth. I can't live without your beautiful mouth, darling."

Polly looked at Helen with wide eyes, then down to where her hand had disappeared into Helen's vulva. She looked back up at Helen.

"Am I doing it right, Helen?"

"Yes, your hand feels wonderful. Now I want you to slowly make a fist of your hand, then just keep going up into me slowly. And kiss me Polly please, now."

Polly stopped looking at Helen's crotch, leant forward and pushed her mouth on Helen's and immediately two tongues swam around in their excited mouths.

Helen's eyes were closed and she moaned as she pulled Polly closer to her.

"Keep going up into me. I'll tell you when to stop."

While Helen spoke, Polly took a quick look at her arm. She couldn't believe how far in it had gone.

"Keep going."

Helen felt Polly's hand touch her womb.

"Yes, yes, Polly. You are there, darling. Just rest for a moment while I feel your beautiful hand in me."

Polly was in awe of what she was doing. She was in Helen's pussy so far with her arm that it was getting close to her elbow. Then Polly felt the first tiny spasm from Helen as she came and for a moment it felt as though her arm was being sucked in even further and then Polly orgasmed too, letting out a tiny scream.

"Oh, Helen you are so beautiful. I love doing this to you."

Helen's face was contorted and she looked at Polly as though she was looking right through her. In a tiny voice, Helen asked Polly to twist her fist very slightly to the left and then back again.

Polly did what she was asked and Helen let out a mighty scream and orgasmed. Polly screamed too and opened her legs wide then slapped them shut again and shuddered.

"Oh God, Helen, I've never felt like this before. I'm so in love with this. Tell me you love it too Helen."

It was as though Helen was asleep with her eyes open, staring into space without seeing. She mumbled something like "I love you, Polly. Please don't stop, Polly".

Polly felt that she should take the initiative. This beautiful older women seemed almost out of it. She was away somewhere else.

Then she decided to take the lead. She ever so lightly twisted her hand back to where it had been before and paused, and then twisted it to the right. Before she had finished, Helen exploded once again and the two of them orgasmed in unison.

It was probably at this moment that Polly, without knowing it, lost her passive, compliant little-girl attitude. Until this point she had happily accepted the role of Celia Ashby's submissive sex slave. She had basked in the pleasure of her mistress and her own accompanying orgasms. Now, for the first time, she felt that she was in charge. She was able to be the provider of the most intimate pleasure to any lover.

Polly twisted her hand inside Helen yet again and Helen screamed and they both came yet again.

When Polly eventually stopped pleasuring Helen, slowly removing her arm and hand from Helen's now limp body, the two women lay down on the sofa, their arms around each other. And when the telephone rang, Polly answered "Miss Ashbee's residence. Yes, Miss Ashbee, yes, okay. I'll tell Helen. She's asleep at the moment," Helen didn't move.

Polly brought a blanket from a cupboard nearby and covered Helen then went out onto the patio beside the pool and lay on a banana lounge in the bright warm sunlight. She closed her eyes and visualised her arm engulfed in the body of her new love, and smiled. Then she turned to let the sun shine on her pussy while her fingers found her clitoris and, while reviewing the vivid images still in her mind, she made herself come once and then a second time.

Helen jumped up from her deep sleep in a panic and looked around. She expected to see Celia or Polly, but neither was in sight and she couldn't hear anyone. She remembered what had happened and a tiny thrill ran through her, but then immediately she wondered what would be said when the mistress of the house got home and found her asleep on the sofa. Why hadn't anyone woken her up?

"Celia won't be home until after six o'clock," came a gentle voice from somewhere outside the french doors leading to the pool. "She rang and apologised and said she would call you tomorrow. I said you were asleep and that I would tell you when you woke up."

Helen shook her head wildly, trying to shake her brain and her hair into some sort of order. Then she smoothed her dress with her hands, trying to look less dishevelled, and walked out into the afternoon sunlight. Polly lay on the poolside lounge beneath a beach towel, wearing sunglasses and a straw hat.

"I'm sorry that I'll miss her. No doubt she will make another date for quite soon." Helen walked to the edge and dipped her hand in the water and splashed her face. There was silence but for the sound of doves in the big pine tree near the fence.

"I'm not sorry that you will miss her."

Polly hadn't moved since Helen arrived.

Helen was silent. She was trying to fathom what Polly meant.

"I don't want to share you with Celia."

Again Helen remained silent. Did Polly see her as a threat, a rival for Celia's affections?

"Polly, Celia loves you very much. She has told me so. There is no way that I could ever replace you in her affections. She's totally into you, so stop worrying about sharing her with me. To Celia, I am simply a friend with benefits. I think that's the correct modern description. Besides, I am totally in love with my husband Frederico, and I have a female friend whom I adore."

Helen turned and faced Polly's stretched out body.

"And now you have me, Helen," said Polly. "I'm in love with you and you won't be able to give me up. I won't let you."

Helen stared at the super gorgeous young thing declaring her love. Casually, Helen reached over and slid Polly's towel from her body. Then she lightly ran her fingers all the way down from Polly's breasts to her her toes and watched the girl involuntarily arch her back.

"I don't want to give you up Polly. I'm in love with you too."

"But how will we see each other? I don't want to only see you here with Celia. I want to have you for my very own." Polly's gasping voice was very clear and almost strident.

"You work here three or four days a week. Is that right? What do you do on the other days?"

"I'm studying at university. I work from home some of the time and I'm at classes a couple of days."

"So can we meet up? At my place, perhaps? I have the house to myself most weekdays and some weekends."

Polly's voice changed. She had sat up and removed her glasses and was suddenly more animated.

"Oh yes! I would love to do that, Helen. And even though I live at home with my mother she is often away on business, sometimes for a whole week, and I have the place to myself."

"There! Sorted already! We will be together exactly as we want to. Now, if there is any problem it is only our relationship with Celia that needs thinking through. I can never be dishonest with her and so I will have to think about what I am to say and do. By the way, Polly, I don't even know what you are studying. In fact, I know nothing about you. What you do in your spare time, for instance?"

Polly laughed. "I'm into horses, and animals generally, and for that reason I'm hoping to become a vet. I go riding with a girlfriend most weekends when I'm not volunteering at a local animal welfare centre. I sometimes socialise with Mum and her friends. There is always something going on, usually involving pool parties with her workmates or clients."

"Great! Now I know a lot more about you. But what about boys? Do you have a boyfriend?"

Again Polly laughed.

"You can imagine that, since working here, I have become a little more worldly, or should we say sexually aware. I do like some boys and older men that I meet and I do have thoughts about some of them. I haven't yet had a cock in me though. Truth is, I prefer girls."

Helen was fascinated to hear about Polly's other life and felt slightly guilty that she hadn't taken more interest in that side of things. But then she told herself that they had only just discovered each other and their intimacy so far had been exclusively about making love.

"So Polly? Do you have a special girlfriend that you can be intimate with? It sounds as though you need one."

"Belinda, my horse-riding friend started kissing me a lot and we used to cuddle up in the feed room at the stables. I got quite turned on by her. We would put our hands inside each other's shirts to touch each other's breasts while kissing and sucking each other's tongues."

Helen was intrigued. "And are you still lovers, Polly? Should I worry that you are going to ride off into the sunset with Belinda?"

Polly screamed with laughter.

"Not going to happen Helen. The stablehand got to her. She said he has a big cock just like some of the geldings get when they are brushed and very relaxed, and she wants to settle down with him and make babies.

"Belinda sometimes grabs me and sticks her tongue in my mouth and mumbles something about missing me, but that's it. I don't do anything back to her. Since being with Celia I've changed, and I don't go looking for new experiences."

Polly smiled and suddenly blushed.

"Well, that is not quite true, Helen, is it?"

Helen put her head back and laughed out loud.

"No, it's not, young lady! Thank God."

Watching Polly blushing was a turn on for Helen and she secretly looked forward to seeing her sweet new love blush more often.

"People can love more than one person, Polly. The intensity of their feelings might be different for each of the lovers in their lives. There is a woman friend of mine whom I love most dearly but in all our time as friends we have never laid a finger on each other.

"At the other end of the scale, the sexual excitement with a lover can be overwhelming and lead us into treacherous territory and eventually to unhappiness. This happened to me when I was your age and it affected me for a long time afterwards. Finding the balance is the key to our sexual happiness."

There was silence while they pondered the questions that life was currently serving up to them.

Polly had sat up and removed her glasses.

"What will I do, Helen? I want to be important to you. How will I deal with these feelings, this jealousy?"

"Polly, dearest, today you made love to me in a special way that I have not experienced with anyone. I won't let you go either."

Polly stood up and took off her hat. She came and sat beside Helen and rested her head on Helen's shoulder and sobbed. Helen waited a little while, then lifted Polly's head and kissed her gently. She then returned the girl to her shoulder and took both her hands.

"We lit a fire today and we mustn't let it get out of control and burn us. Each of us must control the feelings that can result in jealousy. It is such a destructive force.

"Seen from my point of view, you being such a beautiful young woman must result in your having many suitors – both men and women – which means that I must accept that I will one day lose you to a man and babies, or a younger woman who sweeps you off your feet.

"If we can plan our lives, things can be so much more enjoyable.

"Just so you know where I am at this moment, even though I'm very much in love with you, I'm thinking ahead. In particular I'm thinking of Freddy and Alice. If you were to like them and they liked you, then could you cope with being shared between us? It doesn't have to be a choice between you and them, but rather it would be about loving ourselves and others."

Silence prevailed. The sun sank further and the air turned cool. The two women went back into the house.

"Do Freddy and Alice know about you and Celia?"

Polly was hungry for information and Helen chose her words carefully.

"Yes, they are a little bemused and watching my movements with interest. I keep them informed simply by telling them that I like someone and it's early days. This doesn't happen very often, so I don't want you thinking silly things about me. Oh yes, and I always offer to share any new love, but so far it hasn't happened. I and the other two are very moral, good people. They both know that most of my early life was spent with women and darling Freddy understands my need for female company. He is also a wonderful lover. I so want you to meet both of them."

Polly looked up at Helen. Her eyes were dry and the sparkle had returned.

"What happens now?"

"You sexy little bitch. Kiss me like you love me, right now."

Polly's eyes lit up even more and she smiled for the first time and pushed Helen down onto the carpet and jumped on top of her, kissing her and grinding her belly against hers. Helen ran her hand up inside Polly's legs and fingered her.

In a few moments, they both shuddered and collapsed, cuddling and kissing and murmuring "I love you."

––––

It was the day before Helen and Mary would meet in Helen's studio for their monthly "quality time" as Mary called it. Helen was restless and she wasn't sure why.

She had taken on a new lover, the very young Polly who, under instruction, had made Helen very happy. She thought that she should do more with some of the women she loved. She was the experienced, imaginative one, the initiator – the woman who would dream up things to add to everyone's pleasure as well as her own.

As Helen thought about her meeting with Mary the following day, she realised that there was something she wanted to do with Mary, which she believed could benefit all her lovers.

She telephoned Mary.

"Hi Mary! It's me. No, I'm not ringing to cancel. Of course I want to see you, you silly thing. No! What I wanted to do was to put you on notice that I've decided to ask you to do something different tomorrow, but I'm too embarrassed to tell you what it is. We've never discussed it before. No, I can't tell you now either. Just wanted you to be forewarned that your lady lover might be kinkier than you thought. That's all. No! I'm not giving you a clue. No! I'm hanging up. Love you and see you tomorrow."

Helen smiled inwardly and thought how her loving husband Freddy might well get a present out of this, if it all worked out.

––––

Mary was already at the studio when Helen got there. They both kissed and embraced each other.

"Are you going to tell me what this special thing, is or do I have to chase you around the room with your little flagellator up there on the wall. It's 'tell Mary' time."

Helen hugged and squeezed her large lover and sat her down beside her on the bed.

"Well, it's like this, Mary. There is something I like done to me that I find particularly exciting. My darling Freddy understands and happily gives it to me pretty regularly, and that is wonderful, but I'm a bit greedy and I would like to have more of it. I haven't known how to ask you for it, Mary, fearing you might think badly of me."

Mary stared at Helen wide-eyed, all the while clutching Helen's hands.

"Darling, what is it you want from me? You know I'll do anything you ask."

Helen took a deep breath.

"I want you to bugger me, Mary. Shag my bottom. I've bought a smaller strap on dildo designed just for that purpose. Anal sex is something I crave, Mary. There! I've said it."

Mary's jaw dropped. She was speechless. What Helen had just said was taking her a few moments to process.

"Say something Mary. Put me out of my misery."

"Helen. This might surprise you and I've never told anyone until now, but I've always wanted to try it but never knew how to go about getting started.

"A woman where I worked before I was married talked about it one day. She was very good-looking and looking back now, I think I probably had a crush on her but didn't know it. We lived quite close to each other and would catch the bus home together.

"Linda was her name. She told me that her new boyfriend was giving it to her every which way and when I asked her how many ways there were, she laughed and pointed to her mouth, between her legs and then, half turning, she pointed to her bum.

"When I asked which one she enjoyed the most, she giggled and pointed down behind her. Ever since that moment I've wondered about it and longed for a chance to try it, but the opportunity has never arisen.

"Helen, after all these years you might make that wish come true. If I work out how to do it to you, Helen, would you please be so good as to try and do it to me afterwards? I'll try not to make a fuss and if it's not for me at least I'll know I've had a try."

Now it was Helen who was speechless. Mary's answer had been totally unexpected.

"I am so surprised, Mary. I never dreamt that you even suspected that people did such things. I misjudged you entirely. You have made me so happy, I feel like crying. My dear Mary is going to liberate us both. I'm so excited."

Mary looked at Helen lovingly. "Tell me what we do next, Helen. I'm ready when you are."

Helen laughed. "I guess we simply do our usual loving sexy things, darling. Once we are warmed up, I will open up my back door for you and, hopefully my bottom will seduce you and revel in your loving attention."

"Oh, Helen? You make it sound sexy just by talking about it."

Mary fell backwards onto the bed, dragging Helen on top of her. Then she ran her hand down Helen's back and pulled her skirt up. She slid her hand into Helen's panties and ran her fingers down the crack of her bottom, lightly touching and resting on her tiny wrinkled orifice murmuring, "you are going to be mine, all mine."

Helen giggled. "Oh Mary. You are a dream come true."

Helen interrupted their passionate kissing and grinding of each other's bodies against each other and announced to Mary that she was ready.

Then she reached under a pillow and handed Mary a bottle of lubricating oil. From the drawer beside the bed she produced a small pink strap-on dildo. She licked the end of it provocatively as Mary watched. Then Mary took hold of it as Helen was still mouthing it and moved it gently in and out of Helen's mouth before taking it and putting it in her own mouth.

Helen smiled lovingly at Mary with that special pleading come-hither look as she watched Mary attached the dildo to her waist. Helen then rolled over, and pushed herself up onto her knees, pushed her bottom upwards, swaying slowly from side to side.

"I'm ready, my love. Come and bugger your lover. I want to feel you heaving up and down on my bottom, you sexy bitch. Please pour in some lube and get your legs between mine, right now."

In seconds, Mary had squeezed lubricant into Helen's anus and onto the dildo. Then she slipped in a finger and wriggled it about.

"Oh, Helen? This is so exciting."

Mary positioned herself between her lover's beautiful legs up close to her now wet perfumed rear and gently slid the slippery dildo into her pink, glistening and pulsating love hole.

"Yes, Mary! Yes, you darling! I can feel it and it is wonderful. Shag me my sweet. I might make a noise and call you names as you get going but don't worry. It's because I'm in heaven."

Mary groaned appreciatively. "I'm already calling you a randy bitch, Helen. And I couldn't be more randy myself."

"Just fuck me, you big beautiful slut. Give it to me now, hard. Oh! Oh! Yes, you are such a slut, Mary. You've never had me like this before, have you, you slut? You are very naughty. This poor bottom will never be safe from you again. You will want it again won't you Mary. You do like it, don't you sweetheart. Say you like it."

Mary's heaving buttocks increased momentum.

"Yes, I love it. I've orgasmed once already just from starting to fuck you, you dirty little whore. How could I not want to push you over and get into your bum? Of course I will want to do this; for ever, Helen."

Helen was now making gurgling noises as she murmured "Yes, Yes, Oh yes! Harder you beautiful bitch. Oh yes, Mary! You can fuck me like this any time you want to. Oh my God! You feel so good, you sleazy slut. I love you, you randy bum-fucker. Just don't stop. Don't stop. I'm coming, I'm coming. Yes, Yes, Aah!"

Helen and Mary lay side by side holding hands and catching their breath after their lengthy first anal session.

"You are so good at this, Mary."

The two women laughed.

"I must have a natural talent then, Helen. I hope it works both ways. I'm a little bit nervous about my first lesson. You must be patient with me, darling. Can old bitches learn new tricks? You know what they say."

They both laughed. Then Helen slid her hand under her lover's very large backside and touched her bottom hole with an oily finger. Then she gently slid it in and slowly moved it about.

"You will be fine, darling. And if you don't like it the first time, we can always try little sessions occasionally, just for my sake. My thrills come first of course, you naughty girl."

On Helen's instructions, Mary rolled over and got up onto her knees. Helen slipped a fresh condom onto the dildo and strapped it on and positioned herself between Mary's legs, surveying her lover's magnificent backside. Then with a hand on each buttock, she moved them apart so that she could see her target. She dribbled oil on to Mary's anus and then slipped in an index finger. Mary gave a little start and took a sharp intake of breath in anticipation of what was to follow.

Helen moved her finger slowly round and round in Mary's bottom and then, when there had been no suggestion of discomfort from Mary, she oiled the dildo and slipped the first inch or two into the place for which it was intended. Then she pushed it in further and began to move backwards and forwards.

Helen loved the feeling of Mary's soft buttock cheeks flapping against the lower part of her belly and the wet, smelly pussy hair of both women rubbing together reminded her of the intense orgasm she had experienced when Mary pushed in hard in those last moments.

"I'm going to push it right in now, Mary. Hope you're comfortable with that my darling?"

"Very comfortable," came the reply.

"And then I'm going to shag you good and proper, you voluptuous whore."

"Be my guest, slut slave. I'm loving it so far. Don't hold back Helen. I'm into it already. It feels great. I'm just waiting for my arse-fucking slut to get into it properly and stop worrying about me."

Helen slapped a buttock to let Mary know who was boss.

"Oh! Oh! Yes, all right! I'm ready for anything. Forget about me. Just do what you want with that pink prick thing."

Helen began a serious shagging of Mary's delightful backside, and as she did so the idea ran through her head that, if Mary really did enjoy this, it would be a wonderful present for both Freddy and Mary should the opportunity arise.

Helen experimented. Sometimes she climbed up higher and pushed downwards and at other times she moved down and pushed up. Mary seemed to respond more excitedly when Helen pushed down and Helen settled on that as their preferred movement.

Helen was now forgetting about Mary, concentrating instead on her own needs. She started by biting Mary's shoulders. Then she slid a hand underneath the two of them and fondled Mary's pussy. "Oh God! Yes, please my love!" Mary gasped.

It was not long before Mary screamed.

"Oh God! Yes, Yes, Yes!"

Then Helen joined in Mary's orgasm with a giant one of her own.

Mary buckled and lay on her stomach. But Helen wasn't finished yet.

"No, slut. You can't get away that easily".

Now that Mary was lying flat, she changed hands on Mary's clit and spread the fingers on her other hand around the back of Mary's neck and squeezed it tight, pushing her face down forcefully into the bed. At the same time, she pushed the pink prick especially hard into Mary's arse. Mary screamed.

"You fucking slut? Oh, God, Yes, Yes! Oh God! Yes, my bum and pussy belong to you, Helen. Oh my God! Fuck me, fuck me, oh yes. You're fucking me silly, Helen."

Helen fell to one side, pulled Mary's face around to hers and pushed her tongue into Mary's mouth, wildly rubbing her own clitoris at the same time. Then Helen screamed "Mary! Yes!" as she came, pulling Mary on top of her. They pushed their saturated pussies against each other and both women came again amid screams of passion and delight.

For these two lovers, bottom play was now firmly on the agenda.

It was only a few days after Helen became Poppy's lover when Celia Ashbee called to make another day and time for the two to get together. Her voice sounded normal enough and Helen wondered if she knew about her and Polly. Then Celia mentioned it.

"Darling, I know about Polly's strong feelings for you and I just want you to know that I am happy for her and for you. It's to be expected that young things will come and go in one's life as they mature and discover the world.

"After she confessed her feelings for you, I assured her that I still loved her and you very much and was happy for both of you. She broke down and cried, then immediately perked up and demanded a cuddle in the sitting room.

"I don't need to tell you that the remorseful but unrepentant girl did her utmost to make me happy, and she certainly did. So I should probably thank you for that, darling."

"Now, about us getting together, Helen? Given the new situation with you and Polly, I thought it only proper that you and I get together on one of her days off, so I'm suggesting you come over next Thursday or Friday. Either day suits. What do you think?"

Helen was excited and relieved to discover that her relationship with Polly was out in the open. This was great news.

"Thanks for being so understanding, Celia. I appreciate it. I know that she loves you too and I can only think that Polly's ability to share is all down to your training.

"Thursday will suit me fine. I hope Miss Ashbee will be as pleased to greet her little Helen as little Helen will be to be asked to sit on her knee."

There was much laughter from the other end.

"You're making me wet already little girl. Miss Ashbee will definitely be waiting. See you around ten-thirty. And if you are a minute late my dear, she will no doubt want to punish you."

It was Helen's turn to laugh out loud. Then speaking in her exaggerated schoolgirl voice, she said, "Oh Miss Ashbee. Please, please don't punish me. I'll try not to be late."

Little Helen was indeed late arriving at Celia's house, on purpose of course. Celia opened the door and the two women immediately fell into each others arms, mutually groping and tongue-sucking and looking longingly at each others faces, legs and feet. Then Celia spun Helen around, pinned her against the wall and slammed her abdomen against Helen's backside.

"I told you not to be late and you are. Come with me now. Miss Ashbee is waiting for you and she is not happy."

Celia took Helen by the hand and dragged her to the sitting room and closed the door. Then she dragged off Helen's top and skirt, handling her roughly, and within minutes Helen found herself lying over the piano stool pleading for forgiveness. Then Miss Ashbee inflicted her disciplinary hands on Helen's naked backside and Helen's screams drowned out any other household sounds.

Unknown to the two women inside the room, someone had an ear to the door. Aurora stood and listened to Helen's final screams of "Yes! Yes!" as she palmed her pussy in anticipation.

It was Aurora's monthly pasta-cooking day and she had stuffed her large knickers with sweet-smelling herbs. But there was something else that Aurora definitely wanted to sniff.

It was not long before Celia and Helen had fulfilled themselves and were reclining on the sofa, happily holding hands. Celia announced that it was tea and cake time.

"Do we serve ourselves as Polly isn't here?"

"No, darling. It's Aurora's pasta day today and she said earlier that she would be more than happy to serve my guest."

Celia went and pulled on the thick cord that hung from the ceiling. She pulled it three times, which she explained was the code for the request for cake and tea. Helen watched the beautiful woman walk across the room in her underwear and knew that this little Helen hadn't finished with her teacher yet.

Celia came back and slipped on her skirt and top.

"Pop your dress back on, darling. We don't want to confuse the staff do we?"

With both women looking gorgeous and very proper, Helen wondered about Aurora.

Was Celia's story about her true? Did she really have a beard of black hair between her legs and a giant clitoris? Maybe Celia was making up stories, including the one about her previous maid and the gardener. Now that Helen thought about it, it did all seem rather bizarre. And Celia was a great storyteller.

There was a knock at the door, then it opened and Aurora entered. She came across the room and placed a tray of cakes, a teapot and cups and saucers on the low table at the end of the sofa.

"Thank you, Aurora. Aurora, this is my friend Helen. Helen! This is Aurora whom I'm sure I've told you about."

Helen looked up at the strong and beautiful Italian woman. She was impressive to say the least. One would have to say that she was large in every respect, but everything was in proportion and Helen was reminded of the voluminous women often depicted in paintings by great artists.

Aurora's eyes sparkled and her aquiline nose and high cheekbones gave her face a classical beauty. Her skin colouring was a beautiful dusty tan, and the dark shadows around her eyes added to their intensity.

"Aurora! I'm so pleased to meet you. I've wanted to meet you since Celia first told me about you."

Celia beamed up at the large woman.

"Do you have time to join us for a little while? I so want to share you with my guest."

Aurora smiled and said she could and seated herself in a big chair close by. Sitting down pulled her tight black skirt even tighter, showing her large legs and a magical, sensual view of the dusky flesh peeping above the tops of her stockings.

Helen moved herself about on the sofa and crossed her legs, offering a similar view to her lady friends. She already felt randy from the spanking Celia had given her. Helen noticed a strong smell of herbs in the room. She felt a new wetness spreading through the crotch of her panties and a wonderful feeling of anticipation.

"Aurora, my love. Can I show my friend what you have hidden between your legs? When I described you to Helen, she was very excited. Would you stand up and come closer and lift up your skirt?"

Aurora offered an all-knowing smile.

"She looks like she would enjoy more than just a look, Miss Ashbee. I'll take off my skirt. That will make it easier."

Aurora stood up and unzipped her skirt and let it drop to the floor then stepped out of it. She was wearing black silk underpants. She stepped forward and stood in front of Celia.

"Do what you always do to me, Miss Ashbee. You know how much I enjoy it."

Then she looked at Helen.

"Feel free to help her, Helen. I would like that too."

Without another word being spoken, Celia reached forward and dragged Aurora's silk pants down over her ankles. Aurora stepped out of them and moved forward to stand between Celia's legs, which were already wide apart.

Helen gasped.

"Oh my God, Aurora, you are so beautiful."

As she spoke, she moved off the sofa, dropped to her knees and knelt beside Aurora's lovely legs. The smell of herbs was wonderful and she could smell something else, something familiar, the warm sweet smell of Aurora's sex. Celia reached for Helen's hand and lifted it up to touch Aurora between her legs. Helen gasped.

In this giant tangle of black curly hair, an unusually large bright red clitoris appeared and stood out, looking for a loving pair of lips.

Celia leant across, lifted Helen's face, leant forward and kissed her.

"Aurora and I want you to share this special gift Helen. Put it in your mouth, darling, and suck it. Aurora will love you for it."

Helen looked up at Aurora's smiling face.

"Can I show you my breasts too?"

"Yes, Aurora, we want to see all of you, including your delicious backside," whispered Celia.

Helen stared upwards with her mouth open and her lips about to spread themselves around Aurora's clitoris.

Aurora had unbuttoned her top and thrown it on the floor behind her. Then she unbuckled the fastener on her bra and threw it away also.

Helen's world was turning upside down with excitement. Aurora's clitoris was pulsating in her mouth like a little penis looking for attention. Above her, Aurora's huge chest stood out firm and rounded and two giant orbs offering two very large stiff nipples were also begging for attention.

Celia saw that things should change and asked Aurora if she would kindly lie down on the carpet so that both of them could better get at all of her charms.

"But first, dearest woman, just turn and show us your beautiful backside."

Helen let go of Aurora and moved back as Aurora pirouetted to display her giant buttocks. She knelt down and wiggled her bottom at the other women, provocatively. Then she rolled over on her back, and two excited randy women collapsed on top of her. Within moments Celia was gurgling on giant stiff nipples and Helen's mouth was back, sucking and slurping on Aurora's enormous clitoris.

Now it was Aurora's turn to have what she wanted. Two beautiful wet sweet-smelling cunts, one in each hand, to do with as she wished.

Only Serge, Aurora's husband, could raise so much excitement in her at this moment. When he first came home from work each afternoon, and once he had showered and then removed Aurora's knickers and presented his hard robust cock to her, she knew exactly what to do for her husband.

First she would suck it. Then, with the addition of a little olive oil, she would lead his big cock to her welcoming bum or her cunt, and then she would enjoy this bull of a man in his quest to fulfil his matrimonial responsibilities. He and she never tired of their lovemaking.

With Helen sucking Aurora's clit and biting her nipples, along with a very lascivious well-built woman clutching two soaking cunts, these three women were in heaven together.

Having a new hand feeling her up was exciting for Helen. And it being a new hand that knew its way around her pussy, especially so.

Suddenly, she felt a pair of strong hands around her waist and before she knew it she was on her knees. Celia was suddenly kneeling in front of her with her glorious smile. She looked into Helen's eyes and whispered softly to her.

"Aurora wants to fuck us now darling. She'll start by buggering us with her clit – something she loves – then she'll have us with one of the toys from the music stool. She knows where they are."

At that moment Aurora spat on Helen's anus and shoved her engorged clitoris into the freshly lubricated hole quite roughly. Then she was still.

Helen was content with what was happening, appreciating that this was never going to be anything like Freddy's big cock getting into her at home. But then the little penis-like thing began to pulsate and she relished the sensation, looking back over her shoulder and seeing Aurora's smiling face just as the large woman orgasmed, so obviously happy with what she was having.

Then hands cupped Helen's breasts and she turned and saw the radiant Celia kneeling beside her, her bum in the air, awaiting her turn with Aurora. Moments later, Aurora left Helen and climbed onto Celia and Helen watched excitedly as the two women rubbed against each other and again Aurora suddenly pushed in harder and orgasmed. Helen realised that she was so hot for Aurora that the she could have her in whatever way she wanted.

Helen didn't need to wait very long. Aurora grabbed her once again and rolled her onto her back and pushed her legs apart. Then Helen felt a squeegee bottle on her pussy and lubricant being squeezed in. She opened her eyes and stared at the large, smiling Italian beauty between her legs, brandishing Celia's largest dildo.

Aurora rubbed the head of the strap-on against Helen's pussy then shoved it in, working her way deeper very quickly. Helen gave a little scream, then settled back as Aurora pushed and shoved and worked the instrument as if she was ploughing a field. Aurora grabbed Helen's ankles and lifted her legs up high, giving Helen the extra thrill of seeing her own legs waving in the air above her.

Aurora turned her head and bit Helen's ankle; then she looked down, smiling in a way that told Helen that Aurora was truly in heaven as well.

Helen began to gasp as this amazing woman shagged her. If Aurora was a little brutal, it worked for Helen and it was only a couple of minutes before she thrust herself upwards and screamed "Yes Aurora! Yes, Aurora! Fuck, fuck, fuck!"

Aurora yelled something in Italian as she exploded, then she fell forward onto Helen and pushed her tongue into Helen's mouth. Helen welcomed her and their mouths energetically sucked each other.

All the time this was going on Celia was behind Aurora, fondling her big beautiful buttocks, kissing them, licking them and pushing her finger into her anus, and when Aurora orgasmed and then fell forward onto Helen, Celia fastened her mouth on Aurora's newly exposed clitoris and sucked it. Then Celia pushed a hand underneath Helen and fingered her while she wrapped her other hand around the dildo still inside Helen, rocking it gently backwards and forward.

Helen and Aurora both came again.

Now it was Celia's turn.

When Aurora had finished shagging Celia, and Helen had enjoyed licking and biting Aurora's magnificent bottom, all three ladies moved up onto the sofa.

Aurora sat in the middle, her massive legs stretched out before her, wide apart. Her nipples were still very erect and she pulled both women's heads to her breasts and commanded them to bite her.

Aurora's mass of pubic hair and her protruding clitoris were a sight to behold and neither Helen nor Celia could ignore it. Each took a turn kneeling in front of Aurora with her head buried in Aurora's saturated curly carpet while lightly fingering and gently sucking her now very red clitoris.

Every few minutes, Aurora would arch her back and scream in

Italian as she enjoyed yet another orgasm and then she would pull one of whichever womens head was available to her, and mouth and suck her feverishly.

Aurora announced suddenly that she had pasta to prepare.

"You bad girls have seduced me and kept me out of my kitchen. Next time we are together I shall punish you both and you will scream for mercy."

Aurora stood up, collected her clothes and walked out of the room like the tall, upright, naked primitive goddess that she was. Celia and Helen looked at each other.

"Hope you enjoyed that, Helen."

Helen reached over and drew Celia into her arms and the two lovers kissed.

"I enjoyed it immensely, Celia, my darling woman. I will never forget it. Thank you."

Caroline knocked on Helen's studio door and when a voice called "Come in" she entered. Caroline wore a blouse and skirt and white socks and sandals and she had put on lipstick. Helen stared at her visitor and patted the bed, beside which she was sitting.

She had deliberately dressed in a simple light summer frock and sandals, wanting to recapture those moments years back when she would have visited the Bennett home on a hot Sydney day.

Caroline looked at Helen. Helen's choice of clothing worked for Caroline and she vividly recalled past images of the then twenty-some-thing-year-old Helen she so adored.

"Why did you never touch me all those years ago, Helen? You must have known that I ached for you. I was so in love with you and you just treated me as a child. Well, here I am, and I'm no longer a kid and I'm still in love with you."

Helen leant across and gently kissed Caroline's red lips then leant back, still looking into the younger woman's eyes.

"What would you have liked me to do Caroline? Where did your adolescent fantasies take you? Tell me, darling."

Caroline buried her face in Helen's chest and sobbed.

"I so wanted you to fondle me, anything. I wanted you to grab me and push me against my bedroom wall and put a hand between my legs and kiss me and stick your tongue in my mouth, then push me onto the bed and pull off my panties. Oh Helen, I was desperate for you."

Helen held the sobbing Caroline tight with one arm while her other hand gently rubbed the girl's back.

"I had fantasy's about you too, Caroline. I thought about you all the time, thinking of you coming home from school and finding me in your bedroom and me making you take off your uniform. Then I fantasised about making you take off your panties and ordering you to sit on my knee. Yes, darling, I thought about you a lot."

Caroline lifted her head to look at Helen and her jaw dropped and more tears welled up.

"Oh Helen, did you really have those thoughts? Oh God! You did think about me."

Helen held Caroline as she shook. Then she lifted her head and kissed her on the lips. There was a long silence before Helen spoke.

"We are older now, but I still enjoy thinking about you in the way I did then. I think we can enjoy each other and find wonderful things to do by simply remembering ourselves as those randy little sluts we longed to be back then and fantasising how it could have been."

Caroline looked at Helen and smiled.

"Oh yes, Helen. Please, let's be those two young girls who really just wanted to be hot together."

Helen rolled Caroline over so that she lay face down on the bed. Then Helen put her hands around Caroline's ankles and dragged her to the edge of the bed. She lifted Caroline's skirt up and stared at her white cotton-covered bottom and her legs.

"God! You sexy little bitch. You are so beautiful. Are you sure your mum and dad are away for the day?"

Caroline groaned with excitement at this imagined voice from long ago, and whispered in her pretend little-girl voice, "Yes Helen. There is no one home."

Caroline felt Helen's fingers slip under the top of her knickers and trembled with excitement as they slid down over her legs and feet.

"You are such a beautiful little bitch. Now get up on the bed on your knees, girl, so that I can slap your bottom and play with your pretty little pussy."

Caroline moved quickly to fulfil her mistress's wishes, spreading her legs a little as she did so.

"I've waited a long time for this, young lady. Now that you are at last old enough, I'm going to visit you in your bedroom every week when you get home from school and when your folks are out, and lick and suck your beautiful little pussy until you come on my mouth."

Helen bent and shoved her face between Caroline's legs. She opened her mouth wide and fed on the slippery young cunt that was waiting for her, listening to the loud moans of her fantasy schoolgirl Caroline.

"Now girl, are you ready for me to make you come? I want you to do that for your slutty Helen. Then, when I've finished fingering you, I will let you suck your first cunt. I know you've dreamed of it for a long time while you played with your randy self. Think about it now girl. Think about my super wet pussy between your lips. Imagine how you will go looking for my hard little clit. You randy little slut, you've made me very wet already and my pussy needs your attention. Are you ready?"

Caroline screamed out her answer.

"Yes, I'm ready to come now. Please don't stop, Helen. Do it to me!"

When Caroline cried out and orgasmed, Helen joined her and together they bucked and arched their backs, yelling each others names as they came.

Then Helen laid Caroline on the bed and gently licked her inner thighs.

"Now suck me, you darling girl."

When they had exhausted themselves and taken turns rubbing against each other's bellies, they lay back, holding hands and with their heads turned towards each other, staring into each other's eyes with glazed smiles.

"That so worked for me, Helen. You've fulfilled a missing moment in my life. I will love you forever."

Helen squeezed Caroline's hand.

"It definitely worked for me too, darling. I will want to do that again sweetheart, if you don't mind. I hadn't realised how good my slutty schoolgirl fantasy could be.

"Don't lose that schoolgirl outfit Caroline."

The two women laughed and kissed.

"You can come into my room and take off my cotton panties anytime, Helen. And you might like to spank me, if I can think of a way to make you angry. Perhaps I'll struggle with you and then bite you."

Helen put a hand down between her legs to touch herself.

"Stop it, girl, or I'll have to start all over again."

They both laughed and kissed and snuggled up.

"And by the way, my dearest new lover, I will also want your grown-up slutty version very very soon, so don't leave the country yet. Two sluts for the price of one, methinks – the schoolgirl and the power-dressed professional bitch."

They rested and closed their eyes, but then Helen opened her eyes and looked over at Caroline.

"Or maybe three for the price of one?"

"What do you mean, Helen?"

Caroline and Helen both stretched and yawned.

"Well, Caroline. This might sound a little odd, but Freddy and I are very honest about our lovers. It's mostly me who introduces him to women and only occasionally has he suggested that I meet someone whom he's attracted to. I should add that I'm usually disappointed in his choices. They are usually not the sort of people that I would be attracted to, so I do not pursue the offer. I still can't work out what goes on in his head when he first meets them. I can only think that even the most discerning men are too easily seduced by tits and legs.

"Anyway, I should add that Freddy's assignations are very rare. I like to think it's because I fulfil all of his needs." Helen gave a wicked laugh.

"This open arrangement is wonderful and the honesty factor gives our relationship added security.

"I mention it because I'm duty bound to tell Freddy about you. Fortunately, he knew we would get together just as soon as we heard that you had arrived in Australia. The way I reacted to the news, almost orgasming in the kitchen and demanding his hand between my legs, left no doubt in his mind that sparks would fly as soon as we met.

Caroline leant over and kissed Helen, murmuring "I love you". "I'm telling you this because, when Freddy knows that we've become lovers, he may feel romantically inclined towards you and suggest you and he have a moment together.

"There will be no pressure on you, I can promise, and you can say, "No thank you". But he has Fridays off and I am usually away that day, so if it's going to happen and you are up for it, I suggest you keep Fridays, late morning, free."

The two were silent while they each thought through what had been said. Then Caroline responded.

"I don't know that my situation is the same, because Roger and I have only recently got together and I wasn't going to tell anyone yet, but it's probably right for me to mention it to you. The agreement between Roger and me is for him to get me pregnant. I want to return to Australia and have a baby, Helen."

Helen turned and sat up and stared at Caroline in dismay.

"And why I'm saying this is that Roger was smitten with you when we all first met and he did not try to hide the fact that he would love to shag you.

"I suppose our relationship could be called open by default. I'm not sure what he thinks about me, but I'm feeling closer to him every day. Who knows, I could fall in love with him.

"He understands that I'm mainly into girls, so that is not a problem. I'm already the lover of his stepsister Jackie and her partner

Miranda in London, both of whom will be moving into Number 21 to share the house with Roger towards the end of the year.

"Incidentally, Roger prefers mature women. He told me about his early experiences at age sixteen when he went to the farm of his widowed aunt, and how the aunt and the woman who cooked for her seduced him. More recently he has been living in a small town on the Italian coast while finishing his second novel and I'm pretty sure, from what his sister told me, that he discovered a plentiful supply of mature Italian women there."

Caroline laughed. "Sorry! That was probably too much information darling."

Helen was propped up on her elbow, keenly watching and listening to Caroline. She was processing what her new lover was saying, mixing images of herself shagging Roger and then thinking of Caroline having Roger's sister and her girlfriend, with the still fresh images of her pretend schoolgirl lover. And then there was the prospect of later having two new, and likely willing, women neighbours.

Helen decided that she would be ready to shag Roger if he showed interest, and she was also thinking about how Freddy might view this situation.

"Wonderful information Caroline, it so helps me to know you better. It also assures me that you are indeed a slutty little bitch. I think a five-minute kissing session is needed right now."

Caroline rolled on top of Helen and their mouths locked in mutual enjoyment.

"I'm looking forward to our grown-up slutty version, Helen. I'm travelling light, but I'm sure there is a garter belt and a corselet in the luggage somewhere, and there is a new pair of heels too. Promise you will play with my suspenders you slut, if I packed them. If not, then my garters with bows."

Helen looked at her partner lovingly.

"Yes, dear, how could I not do all of that? Plus I have to have you satisfy my secret fetish. I want to look at you on your back on the edge of the bed with your bare backside on show, wearing your heels and with your legs high in the air while you twist your ankles and feet."

Caroline thrust her abdomen upwards and whined in her little-girl voice.

"Helen! You're making me hot again. Can we just have a bit more naughty schoolgirl, please?"

Helen sat up on the edge of the bed and dragged Caroline over her knee and lifted her skirt.

"You horny little bitch. How dare you try to seduce me while I'm helping you with your homework. If I didn't know better, I'd think you were trying to get me to lick your pussy. Now take that!"

Helen had experienced a lot of spanking at the hands of her first lesbian lover, Miss Lazarus, and was an expert in administering punishment in varying intensities. As her hand fell lovingly on her victim's bare bottom, Caroline squirmed in an effort to escape and cried out.

"You fucking bitch. That hurts so much. I'm not playing any more. Let me go!"

This caused Helen to slap Caroline's bum a little harder.

"We are not playing games, you little slut. Now open your legs wide so that I can rub your wet little cunt. If you're good and do as you're told, I might let you get up. But only after you've kissed and licked me."

When the two finally rested, Caroline hugged Helen and kissed her on the lips and on her breasts and licked her neck.

"I love you so much."

"I love you too, darling girl. Now! Are we agreed that we should shag each other's blokes? I'm up for it if you are. Haven't tried another cock in ages. But we can't be sure about them. Guess we'll need to check with them first."

"Everything being equal, it sounds like a plan I could work with," replied a drowsy post-orgasmic Caroline.

Helen wasn't sure how a threesome with her new lovers would go. Both Polly and Caroline were beautiful and sexy and she wanted them both to enjoy themselves. The two had just met for the first time at Maude's party and were very obviously into each other, waiting only for Helen to join them, and walk them next door to her house.

There was also the matter of where the three would spend the evening together. Helen's husband Freddy had told her that he and his two lovers, Freya and Sophie, would be using one of the bedrooms at home. Perhaps Helen's studio would do, although it would be very hot from the summer sun. There was also the lounge room.

Helen admitted to herself for the first time that she was extremely tired and unusually, found herself not fully excited by the evening's prospects. She would need to tell them the truth, she thought. Maybe they would be happy to let her just watch them discover each other. That might satisfy her lustful feelings for both of them.

When Helen was at last able to join Polly and Caroline, the pair were in an extreme state of happy excitement and she knew that they both needed each other desperately. She understood the feelings they must be experiencing, better than most people.

"Helen, darling, we've found a room here. There are a couple of empty rooms that were booked but cancelled and Maude told us to help ourselves. She suggested Room 4. Is that okay, Helen?"

"Yes Polly, that sounds great. Are you two ready?"

They both smiled at her and then at each other.

"Well, before we head down heaven's passageway to Room 4, I do have to confess something."

Caroline and Polly looked at each other and frowned.

"Oh God, Polly, Helen has double booked. She's had an offer from that bloody vicar, I bet, and she's going with the cloth rather than our silk knickers."

They all fell about laughing and Helen thought how lucky she was to have such wonderful women in her life.

"No, darlings. I want to confess in advance that I am extremely tired and I'm concerned that I may be of a bit of a dampener on our party. I thought I should mention it now so that you could send me home alone, or you could tuck me up in your bed and let me watch a coming together of two beautiful women who deserve to have their heads between each other's legs. There! I will abide by your decision."

There was silence as what Helen had just said sank in. Then Caroline and Polly looked at each other and smiled and nodded as if they were acknowledging a secret agreement. The two rose from their seats and stood on either side of Helen's chair. Then they lifted her up.

"Just come with us and don't say a word," whispered Polly.

Helen's two lovers escorted her out through the passage door as if she was a prisoner, and once they were inside Room 4 and had dimmed the lights they kissed her in turn and stripped her of her clothes, then dragged her into the bed and tucked her in.

"Now, Helen, we are going to remove each other's clothing and kiss, probably quite a lot, and even make noises, all of which you can watch, or not if you fall asleep. However, both of us will take advantage of you every once in a while and come pushing between your legs for a lick of our love's special spot. Is that clear?"

Helen looked at Caroline sleepily and smiled lovingly.

"And if by chance you do wake up, feel free to lend a hand, Helen," added Polly.

Helen smiled, and closed her eyes and spoke softly.

"Go fuck each other, you slutty bitches. I love you both."

She rolled onto her side and Polly and Caroline stretched out their arms and embraced, then their lips joined and they fell onto the bed with their hands moving about as they lifted each other's frocks and discovered each other's parts.

And when the moment arrived some time later when their two naked bodies were lying on each other and their pussies were still slowly rubbing together, something stirred next to them and a leg pushed itself in among theirs.

Another pussy pushed against them and they heard Helen's sleepy voice.

"If there is anything left over, I'd like some please."

———

Mary had mentioned to Helen that Sophie had gone through a stage of feeling depressed and how she had confided in Mary that she would like to see more of Freddie.

Then Alice had reported a similar story from Freya and Helen realised that it hadn't just been about getting them with child. There was a lot more going on.

Helen also acknowledged that, not having a child of her own was probably the reason she had failed to foresee this situation.

After consultation with Freddy, Helen reached out to Sophie and Freya and invited each of them to spend a night a fortnight in the matrimonial bed instead of her. This added up to a night a week that she would not sleep with her husband.

Sophie had broken down and cried, thanking her and embracing her in a great show of feeling which ended up with both of them naked on the sofa in the drawing room. And Freya reacted by immediately unbuttoning Helen's shirt and begging to be allowed to suck her breasts.

So readily had the three taken to the arrangement, Helen was now wondering how long or even if ever the time would come when they stopped enjoying her husband.

Helen brooded about getting older and losing touch with all her lovers. She was even seeing less of Polly now that she was at vet school full time and plus she was spending more time with her horsey friend Belinda. This liaison had also moved into a new phase where both girls were now members of an exclusive dressage group. And Polly even let slip that her new horsey friend, Clifford, had asked her to visit his parents farm in the Hunter Valley for a weekend.

On the face of it, Helen's world was turning upside down and she was feeling insecure.

When Helen eventually talked to Freddy about how she felt, he told her not to see things so negatively and that everyone loved her. For Freddy, life just moved on and he did his best in every way he could, attending to what he thought was needed most. Now it was babies and their mothers that took up a lot of his thinking.

Helen thought how this wonderful man had become two other women's wonderful man. She knew, deep down that it was her fault for seducing the two girls in the first place and so she was denied the chance to blame something or somebody.

If this feeling of things being lost to her wasn't enough, her neighbour, Mary, seemed less keen to visit her and when Helen asked Mary to pop over the next day for some time together, Mary had begged her to change the day as she had something else on, although she wouldn't say what.

Helen couldn't help wondering what was happening to the world.

It was a week or so after Rosa's birthday and it was after dinner one night, that Frederico dropped a booklet on the coffee table in the lounge and asked Helen if she knew about The Club.

"No, darling. I've no idea what you are talking about my love. Should I know? Are we going to be selling raffle tickets for it?"

Freddy laughed. He had spent the afternoon with Roger and Bertie at their fortnightly coffee and cake session upstairs at the Ampersand Cafe in Paddington.

"Roger told us all about it today. He was employed to write up and design this booklet for the owner. I must say that I was shocked when I heard about it, especially when I found out where it was located. I'm still a bit shocked but I'm starting to sort it out in my head."

Helen looked at her husband quizzically, "What on earth are you taking about, darling. Not much shocks you. The last time was when you discovered you were going to be a father for the second time in a month. Should I be worried?"

Freddy spent the next thirty minutes filling Helen in on what he knew about The Club. While he did this, she inspected the booklet he'd brought home.

"I suppose the biggest shock is that it's all happening just down the road," Freddy said.

Helen was intrigued that such a thing existed and begged her husband for more details and asking questions that he didn't have answers for such as "Did husbands and wives go together sometimes or did they just meet up accidentally at The Club?"

They talked about The Club for the rest of the evening. Freddy related and often repeating all that Roger had told him and said how Bertie had mentioned that he and Rosa knew Desley, the owner and her brother Arnold quite well and that he had also met her mother, who was instrumental in getting Eros Crescent renamed. He said she was a fine woman and he wished her well.

Helen, as did Freddy, had more questions than she or he could possibly think up answers for. But as the night drew on and Freddy opened a second bottle of red wine, the two began to see the funny side of things and make jokes.

"Well, darling. I think we should join and then I will put on a wig and enjoy pretending to be somebody else and letting you seduce me, thinking I was the woman in the next street you've always had the hots for."

Freddy giggled.

"I wonder if she is a member?"

Helen punched him but missed and he caught her in his arms and kissed her.

"I suppose membership would fit into our sharing and caring philosophy. What do you think? I guess it's a matter of how much caring and how much sharing we are prepared to get involved in. As you know, darling. In matters of where one expends energy, I'm a bit stretched at the moment," Freddy managed to say with only the slightest hint of an alcohol inspired slur.

Freddy looked at Helen intently, searching for clues of how she thought about it, knowing full well that she was uneasy about him spending so much time with Freya and Sophie.

Helen smiled at her lovely husband and chose her words carefully.

"Well, I seem to have a lot of time on my hands lately Freddy. My lovers all seem to be pregnant or otherwise engaged. Even Mary is making excuses not to see me and Polly is about to be raced off by a young aristocratic polo-playing lad from the Hunter Vally.

"In truth, my love, I do have a small space in my daily routine for a caring and sharing dalliance. But if we joined, it should be as a couple, don't you think. You might just need an occasional change of scenery? I think the daddy-to-be deserves that. We would need to coordinate our club activities so as not to clash, of course."

Freddy leant back on the sofa and smiled at his true love.

"You know that you will always be the most important woman in my life, Helen. I am sorry if you are going through a difficult period with everyone, including me. I'm not against you joining The Club and if they have a special rate for couples, I'm happy to become a member."

There was a silence as the two considered the situation.

"I'll check it out darling."

"Oh yes, Helen. I forgot to mention that we have to be nominated by an existing member. I suspect Roger can help us there. Check with him first."

It was coincidental that Helen phoned Roger about the club as he and Caroline were talking about it. Helen told him that Freddy had shown her the booklet and they had talked about joining The Club.

"He suggested I call you, Roger. He thought you might be able to take me there as a guest. Is that possible? Would you mind?"

Roger was a little surprised to receive Helen's request, but he told her that he wold be happy to show her around and would tomorrow, Wednesday, at 2 o'clock be okay? Helen said that it would be a good time and then she asked him how Caroline had responded to the subject of The Club and Roger was able to say that the two of them were discussing it when she called.

"Well, I'd better leave you to it. Love to Caroline. Tell her that we will have much to talk about when I see her after our adventure."

Caroline had heard all that Helen had said and was much amused.

"Well, Roger. I'm only away for a short time and you have successfully impregnated someone, shagged the home help, and written a manifesto which could revolutionise western culture as we know it. A girl has to be impressed. Now! When do I get to go to The Club?"

Roger quickly thought about it and replied, "Tomorrow at 2 o'clock be okay with you? You and Helen can share the experience."

Helen and Catherine were excited to see each other and hugged and kissed.

Roger opened The Club door and ushered his lovely ladies into the foyer. Alvie looked up and smiled and Roger introduced her to his two accomplices.

"So good to see you, Roger. I see you've brought your own ladies. Aren't those you meet here good enough for you?"

Everyone laughed and Caroline suggested that now she was back, she would expect that Alvie might see less of him. Alvie went along with the ruse and said how Roger was rather particular and now, having met Caroline, she understood why.

Caroline thanked her and confessed that because she was now pregnant, Alvie might see him more frequently over the coming months.

Roger acted the tourist guide part perfectly, fielding question after question. Even though he had and Freddy had explained much to their partners, as so often happens, things don't sink in so that they both asked how many men could be entertained in the Home Delivery rooms, and both asked him to explain the twelve rows of seating and their designations to better understand how one learnt to shop for whatever it was you were looking for.

Going inside the theatre was the most exciting moment for both of them.

As Roger walked them slowly down the side aisle and their eyes grew accustomed to the reduced light, both Caroline and Helen would touch each other to draw attention to something. Then they watched in awe as a man pushed down the bra on the woman in the seat in front of him and gently levered her breasts out, one at a time before fondling them.

"My God, Caroline. Imagine this on daytime TV."

Just moments later they were looking at a woman who was

staring at the movie screen and seemingly absorbed in the movie. She wore a top coat which was pulled back and exposing her naked breasts, suggesting that the coat was her only piece of clothing. On either side sat a man each with his hand on one of her breasts. But of greater note was the fact that both men's cocks were exposed and erect and being slowly rubbed by the woman in the coat.

"Astonishing! And I thought I'd seen it all. My God. No woman need want for anything every again," said Caroline, holding Helen's hand for reassurance.

When they eventually managed to get further down, the two gasped in unison as they saw two women cuddling each each other in row eight while blatantly exposing themselves to the world.

That was when Helen and Caroline both exclaimed as one, that they wanted to try rows eight or nine to see if they could get some attention.

Roger looked and listened and laughed and then realised that the two were being serious.

"Why don't I leave you here for a little while then? Even if you don't get any takers, you will at least be able to relax and feel the vibes of the place and understand it all a bit better.

Helen and Caroline looked at each other and smiled. Then they told Roger that they thought that this was a good idea. And as they hadn't had any time alone together since Caroline's return, this would be as good a place as any for them to start.

Roger smiled at the two beauties, and said how he would try to find something to do for the next half-hour or so, to which Caroline replied, that she thought she had seen an attractive woman arriving in row six and maybe he should check her out.

Roger turned to retrace his steps and rejoiced that Caroline and Helen had so readily settled into the idea of The Club.

Roger returned and as he approached row eight, he realised that his visitors had indeed attracted their own visitors. It looked as though the couple who were already there when Caroline and Helen arrived, had moved over to join them.

Helen was on her knees with her head buried between the legs of a woman who was bare breasted. The other woman was between Caroline's legs, moving her head rhythmically up and down. Caroline's breasts were also uncovered and each of the sitting woman had a hand on the others breast. It was indeed a restful but exciting scene and Roger didn't want to interrupt it.

Roger met Caroline and Helen as they were slowly making their way up the aisle from where they had been sitting. They were stopping regularly to look at what was going on and when Roger approached, they were silently witnessing an event in row three, The Jungle.

"Oh my God! How many men has she got behind her now?"

"I think it must be four plus the one laying on the seat under her. He's already made his entrance, from what I can see, so I can only guess where the others might be putting theirs."

Roger stood and watched unnoticed as his two companions stared at what was usually a once-a-day event, if that. He thought how good it was that they had seen so much on their first visit.

"We would like to come back here. Helen and I enjoyed ourselves very much, didn't we Helen?"

Then Roger quipped, "Anyone for a cup of tea or coffee?"

"Oh yes. I've tried to call Helen in case she wanted to come but there was no answer. If she comes by looking for me, tell her I'm sorry I missed her but I'll be back at around three or four o'clock."

Then Caroline gave Roger an odd look.

"You might not have noticed but Helen and Frederico are going through a bit of a thing, partly because of Sofi and Freya's wanting to see more of Freddy now they are going to have his babies.

"We talked about it and she said she hoped this jealousy thing she was feeling wasn't going to happen with me and Alice.

"I told her that so far, Alice hasn't acted in any way that seemed remotely possessive. I also said that if she did, it might be different for us because she and I are closer in age than Helen and the two girls.

"I'm mentioning it so that if she shows up, you won't be too blokesy. Bye darling!"

Caroline turned back to look at Roger. She was very relaxed, but offered him an odd look and then smiled.

"Come to think of it, Roger, if she does happen to call in, I'm certain that it would be much appreciated by her and me if you were able to be especially nice to her, seeing how lonely she's feeling. You get my drift, don't you darling. Just a last minuted thought. See you later in the day, sweetheart. I'll try to think of something special to bring home."

Caroline blew Roger a kiss and disappeared.

Roger had just returned to his desk with his cup of coffee when there was a knock at the door and Helen's voice called out.

"Can I come in?"

Roger heard the door close.

"I'm in here, Helen. Come through."

Helen appeared at the door of his office come spare bedroom.

"Hi Roger. It's so lovely and warm in here. Is the girl around?"

Roger looked up and was immediately smitten yet again with the beautiful wife of his best friend, Frederico. This mature woman ticked more of his boxes than he ever thought possible.

A smiling Helen stood in the doorway dressed in a heavy jumper under a see-through poncho. He noticed her tweed skirt and heavy brown stockings and practical brown walking shoes. Her medium length brown hair had been messed up by the violent winds blowing outside.

"You've missed the girls. They've gone of to do pampering or some such thing that men don't really understand. Caroline told me to pass on that she had tried to contact you but without success."

Helen stared at Roger as though trying to read his inner thoughts.

"Never mind. I'll go and put the heater on in my studio and try to get creative. Looks like you are pretty busy, Roger, so I won't interrupt you."

Roger's response was very quick.

"I'd love you to stay, Helen, that's if you would like to. I'm just going through stuff that Desley gave me. She wants me to comment on the things people have left in the suggestion boxes at the club and report back with my thoughts. It could be fun. You might help me, perhaps.

"After that, I'm about to restart a major project for her that stopped because of lockdown, but I'm putting that off for a couple of days until I get more information.

"Please stay. It's warm here and there are comfy chairs and even a bed if you get tired and need to take a snooze. And I will even attempt to make you a perfect coffee if you so desire."

Roger was aware that he was selfishly wanting Helen to be here with him while at the same time, attempting to fulfil Carolin's wish that he be especially nice to her girl friend.

Helen's stare softened and she agreed that his office was probably the right place to be given how cold and windy it was outside.

Helen came in and walked over to the armchair at the end of Roger's desk, and made herself comfortable, laying her arms on the soft chair arms and crossing her legs.

"Have you and Caroline sorted out your wedding arrangements, Roger? The last time I saw the two of you together, she was telling you to sod off. I get the feeling that that is well behind you now."

Roger's face made a tight lipped grimace.

"A man never really know where he stands with a woman. But to answer your question, yes, I think our betrothal will happen in the spring, complete with a full lesbian ceremony and service.

"I suspect I'll be the only man there. Oh no. Freddy will have to be best man of course. I haven't asked him yet. I hope he'll be up for it."

Helen seemed to stiffen in her chair.

"You might like to consider a plan B, Roger. Freddy is preoccupied with his other wives to the point of not having time for anything else."

Roger reminded himself that Caroline had told him that Helen was in a difficult space at the moment. He looked at Helen and smiled.

"Thank you Helen. I'll remember that."

He removed the two clips holding the mens and womens notes from the suggestion boxes at The Club.

"Okay, Helen. Are you ready? I'm going to start by just reading quickly through all of them, then we can go back and address each question in detail.

"Lets start with the women's suggestions."

Helen had responded to the humour of the moment and laughed loudly which encouraged Roger to think that she was likely to relax and enjoy her visit and maybe his company.

Helen got up and came over and stood beside Roger enthusiastically urging him to let her see, "what the girls have to say."

"From the ladies suggestions box, we have;

"Note one: Do condoms get recycled and if so what do they end up as? Signed: Stickyfingers

"Note two: Could we please have deodorant available for sale at the kiosk, particularly men's deodorant? Signed: Nosegay Gertie

"Note three: Could we have a service via the smart card where a woman can book a man for a long session of cock sucking. Men generally are in too much of a hurry to move on to the next bit. Signed: The Pointer Sisters

"That sounds reasonable," Roger mumbled.

"Note four: One man and one woman for extended anal sex sessions in private. Signed: Bottom Draw

"Oh wow! How do I find this woman? My fantasy could be fulfilled after all these years."

Roger heard Helen gasp and looked up at her. Helen was staring at the last entry and then she looked at Roger. She seemed as though she was trying to sort something out in her head. Then she reached down and took Roger's hand in hers and looked at him strangely.

"Is everything all right, Helen?

Roger held onto her hand and looked up at her, waiting for her response.

"I wrote that last one, Roger. I went for a pee just before we left The Club the other day and just couldn't resist adding a suggestion."

The two stared at each other as though they were about to go through a door to an unknown land.

Roger found himself reaching out with his other hand to Helen's leg standing beside his chair. He touched her on her calf and felt the excitement of gently rubbing her stocking covered leg.

Helen let go of Roger's hand and touched his face and looked longingly at him.

"Is that suggestion really what you would like, Helen."

"Oh yes Roger. Oh yes, it really is."

Helen clasped the sitting Roger's head to her bosom as Roger's hand moved slowly up her leg. He didn't want to frighten her or for her to think he was just making out for the sake of it.

"Roger?"

"Yes, Helen?"

"If it is true that we both want the same thing, then I should tell you that at the moment, no matter what I want, I'm feeling quite fragile and vulnerable and could find it difficult to respond to you in the way we both would want. One thing that would help me would be for you to just kiss me, Roger.

"Stand up and kiss me please Roger. I need to sort out my emotions and kissing will do it for me."

Roger stood up and put his arms around Helen, feeling her collapse into him. Then he felt her trembling and heard her sobbing and he pulled her closer. She lifted her head and her eyes shone and she put her mouth on his and the two melted into one another.

After trembling for some time whilst still managing to kiss Roger, Helen moved her head back so that she could look at him.

"I must warn you that I won't be able to stop once we start, Roger. Once I give you my rear you will have me forever. I will want you there and you will want to be there, be it for just ten minutes or for hours on end. If you can give me what I crave then you will never get rid of me."

Helen felt Roger's cock growing in his pants against her belly and she relaxed and smiled and went back to kissing him.

Roger ventured to put a hand down over Helen's thick skirt and massage her backside. Then he lifted her big woollen sweater up to her neck and looked down at her beautiful chest, slowly heaving with emotion. Helen breathed deeply and he noticed she'd stopped trembling. She reached up and moved his head so that she could put her lips back on his and they tongued each other.

"I'm ready, Roger," Helen whispered. "Before you take me anally you will have to fuck me a little bit. It will get things wet for me and I so love to be wet."

Roger heard what Helen said. He didn't want to let her go but he knew he would have to. He wanted what she wanted and they both wanted it now.

Roger reached behind Helen and unzipped her skirt and it fell to the floor. Then Roger held her hand while he stood back to look at her. She was a vision splendid. He turned her around and looked at her backside. Roger was looking at his ideal woman.

Roger knew that he wanted to move on with Helen. He unzipped his pants and removed them along with his boxer shorts and his member stood up tall and straight and Helen stared at it.

"I'm feeling better every moment, Roger. And I can see you are serious. Take off my undies and inspect and touch my rear, Roger. I'm desperate for you to feel me."

Helen reached out and took hold of Roger's cock and whispered to it.

"You are going to heaven and taking me with you. You will become mine and I will become yours."

Helen looked deep into Roger's eyes then she slipped a hand into her knickers and rubbed herself.

"My activities in recent years have only been with women, Roger. This feels very much like my first time and I'm nervous.

"Women accept other womens bodies and behaviour quite easily. So if I tell you that I have a very hairy vagina and that I often make a lot of noise during sex and I sometimes bite people, will that put you off me? Before I can relax, I need to feel secure, Roger. Help me feel secure, you lovely man."

Roger stepped back a little and looked down at Helen's beautiful body. He stared at her strong stockinged legs then with one hand he pushed down Helen's knickers to her knees and uncovered her hairy crotch and with the other he felt her between the legs, bunching her ample bush in his palm.

"How beautiful you are, Helen. And I love your hairy pussy. You know that I've had two years in Italy where hair down here is worshipped, so believe me when I say I will happily worship you. And I should confess that I can be noisey too."

Helen gave a little start and Roger felt her hand grasp him more tightly, and his cock jumped in appreciation.

Helen put her other hand up to his head and pulled his face to hers and opened her mouth and engulfed Roger's lips, then pushed her tongue into him. As she did so she let go of his member and reached down and removed her panties.

"Fuck my bushy cunt first, please Roger. Then you may take my other spot. I want you to fuck it for ever."

Roger moved Helen over to the bed and lowered her, all without letting go of her sweet spot. Then he pushed her legs apart and removed her hand and nestled the end of his prick in her now very wet hairy vagina, and slowly moved it right in. Helen orgasmed immediately murmuring "Already? Oh God!"

The two bodies clasped each other tightly and tongued each other and Helen's body shook regularly with tiny orgasms that she was prone to when excitement overwhelmed her, and which she hadn't experienced for a very long time.

Helen removed her mouth from Roger's. "Oh Roger, this might end up killing me. This is so beautiful I will never want it to end. Spoil me more Roger and tell me that you love me. I promise I won't hold you to anything you say. Tell me you love me and that you love being in my hairy cunt."

Roger needed little prompting.

"How could I not love you, you beautiful sexy bitch? My cock is in paradise. How will I be able to leave it for that other spot at the back. You will still want me in the back, won't you?"

Helen swung her legs around Roger's waist and pulled him into her, then gave a little laugh.

"Oh Roger. You are such a joy. I want you everywhere all at once. But having you in my arse should settle me down. Take it whenever you wish, my darling. Your cock is nice and wet now and my bum is already screaming out for your attention.

"And Roger. If Caroline comes home and finds us like this, don't worry. She put me up to it. She said she was so fed up with seeing me miserable that she insisted that I have you. I love her so much."

Roger had actually suspected something when Caroline had looked at him as she was leaving and how she had commented that she would like him to be especially nice to Helen. "Well, if she does find us, then she will just have to join in," Roger mused.

Roger slowly removed himself from the hairy heaven. Then he kissed Helen lovingly, and lifted up her legs and backside to make her arse easily accessible.

"I want you this way, Helen. I'll role you over later."

Helen wriggled to position herself in readiness, "Yes, sweetheart. I'm ready. Which ever way is fine."

Roger kissed and licked Helen's anus then inserted two fingers and moved them about. Then with both hands, he opened her hole and stretched it a little and peered inside the pink tunnel. Then he entered her, gently at first and then more assertively.

"Oh God! Yes, yes, yes!"

Helen was happy and so was Roger. The tunnel felt wonderful on his cock and he knew that he could spend a long time there, quietly moving his dagger or stiletto as his Italian twins had tutored him.

Roger looked down at Helen's smiling face, both rejoicing in their erotic pleasure.

The two shagged on through the early afternoon with intermittent kissing and shouting. The they rested and Roger brought his new love, cake and ginger beer. Then they looked at each other and Helen rolled over onto her knees again both nodded indicating it was time for more shagging.

"Oh Roger. This is so beautiful. I just want you to shag me forever. Your big cock feels so wonderful. I just want to cry."

Roger rolled Helen over and pulled her up onto her knees and entered her from behind.

Suddenly, Helen burst into tears and sobbed, her body shaking in unison with Roger's shagging motions.

Then Caroline walked through the door.

"Oh my God. How beautiful you both look. But why is Helen crying?"

Helen looked around at Caroline and put a hand out towards her and Caroline responded. She dragged her thick jumper off over her head, unbuttoned her blouse and threw herself on the bed beside her female idol. As she did so, Helen orgasmed for the umpteenth time, dragging Caroline to her and raining tears and saliva on Caroline's bosom.

"I'm so happy, Caroline. Thank you so much. I won't let Roger stop. I hope you don't mind. I hadn't realised how much I needed this moment. He has been so wonderful and I can't stop shagging him. Why don't you lie beneath me and share. I could lick you and you could play with me and him. I would so love that."

Caroline kissed Helen energetically.

"Oh my dearest Helen. Yes please. Let's do that."

Helen pushed her legs apart far enough for Caroline to squeeze between them, then, as Caroline gently fingered Helen's cunt, Helen reciprocated, fastening her mouth on Caroline wet and fluffy special place.

Caroline put her head to one side so that she could peer up at Roger while at the same time, she took his testicles in her other hand. "Love you darling", she called. Then in a semi jocular voice loud enough for Helen to hear, she called out.

"Fuck the bitch, you wonderful man. I can feel you, and it feels as though you are fucking me too. I love it!

"I think you two are cock-in-the arse loving sluts. I think Helen will want this at least once a fortnight. Am I right Helen? Don't bother answering. I know I'm right. We'll arrange it."

Then Caroline arched her back and enjoyed a very strong orgasm triggering the same thing in Helen causing her to give way to her final surrender as she collapsed on top of Caroline, and leaving Roger sitting back with a still hungry cock.

"Sorry, Roger."

Caroline seized the opportunity and rolled herself out and around and pulled her lover on top of her and, gripping Roger's cock firmly in one hand, she led him to her own little door to heaven nestled between her buttocks, and fed him in.

"Finish yourself off there please darling, as hard and as soon as you like. You deserve it, sweetheart. Thank you. I love you."

It was only moments later that Roger orgasmed inside his lover who lifted her body to meet him and cum with him. And Helen added a small scream and her body shook violently in unison with her two loves.

So ended Helen's first of many loving moments with Roger.

Helen was excited watching Roger bugger Caroline who had only recently discovered the joys of anal and of course the two would share their orgasms and Roger in the ultimate loving relationship. Helen loved to touch the two of them when they were making love, Caroline's clitoris and Roger's testicles being much favoured along with breasts and buttocks.

Arrangements were made for Helen to come and stay over on those nights when her husband, Frederico was with either of the two pregnant ladies, Sophie and Freya.

Sometimes Helen and Roger would be given space in the afternoon to be alone but often they would invite Caroline along for the ride and the three would shag for a whole afternoon.

And whilst the double bed was fine for three people making love, after a night of excitement, Roger would remove himself and cross the room to sleep in the single bed leaving the two women cuddled up in their post orgasmic slumber.

Who ever woke up first, went and made and delivered a tray of hot drinks then Roger would join the two women and they would all cuddle up and most times they would fall into a second slumber.

End

CATCH UP

EROS CRESCENT

No one on Eros Crescent remembers exactly the moment when the words COVID-19 or Corona virus were first uttered in their houses. Needless to say, it would first have been heard on a television report and the importance of the message would have taken a few days to sink in.

The world suddenly changed. Words and phrases like lockdown and self-isolation and social distancing were suddenly in the forefront of all conversations as people enacted the requests of government and the nation to act responsibly to assist in the national objective to achieve what quickly became known as flattening the curve.

For Roger, life couldn't have been less affected. His daily routines required only that he rose from his bed, showered and shaved, ate his breakfast, went for a walk, and made sure he had sufficient pens and paper. Although it did impinge on his new paying project.

He had been asked by Desley to write another booklet similar to the one he'd written for The Club, only this was to be for The Dunking, a venue he had not yet visited or, until now, even heard of.

When Desley explained the concept and related what the setting inside the warehouse was like, Roger was very keen to get started. But the arrival of the virus put an end to that project, at least until further notice.

For Caroline and Jackie and Miranda, staying at home was what they enjoyed anyway, that is when they weren't travelling abroad or window shopping or having coffee in cafe's.

All three women had worked in executive positions in London, but moving overseas brought that era to a close, although they had been invited to join similar companies in Australia.

A top of the range coffee making machine was promptly ordered along with a supply of fair trade East Timorese Maubisse, medium blend. Browsing online shops became the new window shopping.

Instagram took on a new importance as the pandemic took hold around the world. Stories and pictures of people in isolation doing amazing and sometime ridiculous things became the rage. Jackie uploaded hundreds of images of the inside and outside of the house, earning the praise of interior designers and architects.

Helen and her husband Frederico were effected in so far as Freddy's job as a flight controller at the airport was soon to be reduced in the number of hours he worked. However, there was no threat to his income as he was on standby as an essential service. But Helen's work as a freelance Human Resources consultant to industry came to a sudden halt. She embraced online conferencing on Zoom but this was no substitute for real hands-on consulting.

Helen was also restricted in her love life, already reduced as a result of her husbands responsibilities to Helen's two lovers who had inadvertently become pregnant to him.

Sophie and Freya now spent a night a fortnight with Freddy. Unable to visit or have visits from her own lovers, Polly or Celia Ashbee, Helen would just have to manage with her next-door neighbour, Mary. And what looked like the answer to maiden's prayer, The Club had been forced to close.

Mary's only loss of employment was her volunteer job at the Salvation Army Opportunity Shop which she would miss very much. She would also miss her sensual workout with her close friend Janice. But most of all, she would miss her newly found excitement at The Club which she had only recently opened.

Her niece and housemate, Sophie, worked at a horse stud and accepted reduced hours and looked forward to doing baby things at home. Because she and Mary lived next door to Helen and Freddy, the two households would have access to each other when needed. And of course, Freddy was to be the father of Sophie's as yet unborn child.

Alice and Frey both lamented the loss of work in their jobs as school counsellors. They both loved their jobs. Both were pregnant and accepted they would be forced to spend more time at home together.

Like most of the others, they had their favourite sex toys for when they weren't knitting baby clothes or doing jigsaw puzzles. And like so many women in lockdown, they visited female friendly porn sites online. The two decided that they would always share these internet session and happily parked themselves on the sofa, transmitting the websites from their phones to the giant television set via a magic little box. This meant that the images were so big that they felt they were in the same room and this proved most enjoyable on many occasions.

Bertie and Rosa were the older folk who were most vulnerable to the virus. They were happy to be isolated although Bertie complained that he would miss his fortnightly get together for coffee and cake with Freddy and Roger.

Bertie complained that he still had much to say on the subject of breaking down the worlds dependance on the "couples model" as he called it.

"Nothing good will happen while we maintain this ridiculous habit of pairing off for life. Firstly, in over half the cases, it doesn't work and people separated or divorced.

"Secondly, it was obvious that people who stayed in these relationships were deeply frustrated by the repressive demands on them of constantly answering to another person.

"Thirdly, paternity and property ownership where the only reasons this system was maintained and with the likely end of democracy as we know it looming, house prices and pension funds and equity investments were likely to collapse.

"And I haven't even mentioned the problems of religion and religious wars."

Rosa looked at him. She loved him dearly but managed always to call him out.

"You haven't mentioned love once."

"Sex and love are two seperate things, my dear. We both know that."

Most of the close friends and relatives knew that Rosa and Bertie had broken up many years ago and taken lovers. Rosa entered relationships with her close girl friends and occasionally, a man.

Sometime later, she and Bertie got back together as a couple, but both maintained their freedom to embark on other relationships if they so chose, and this arrangement worked very well. It wasn't that they were desperate to take on other romantic adventures, but just knowing that they were free to do so, made the difference. They broke up after almost twenty years and had now been together for nearly fifty years.

"It was a necessary pause," agreed the two of them, lovingly.

The two people that were originally going to be living together but in the end chose not too, were Edith and Jessica. But living at different ends of the same street meant that they would not need to forego their times together. And they, like Maude and the others living in number nineteen, had each other for company if and whenever they wanted.

Edith and Jessica had the boys on hand and could also still get a pizza delivered, although it sometimes took a little longer.

But then they learnt that they would now be sharing the boys with the very sexually active Maude and possibly with the two new girls who moved in to number eleven just before the lock down. Jessica and Edith's plans to invite the new girls in for a pizza, were in hand.

Edith still went for her walk on Mount Eros on most mornings where she usually met her friend Chloe and the two, more than not, would spend loving time together in Chloe's secret cave.

It was thanks to the lockdown, that Jessica met Chloe. Edith had long wanted the two to meet so when Jessica was unable to attend classes, she accompanied Edith on her walks.

Jessica and Chloe were instantly friends. Both knew that the other understood Chloe's relationship with Edith. And when the rain fortuitously arrived on their first walk together, all three made haste to the hidden cave and it was only a few minutes before Jessica had Chloe underneath her on the carpet of leaves with Edith dragging first Jessica's then Chloe's shorts and panties off before sitting beside them with her bare breasts available for the occasional grope from both girls.

It was Desley who had the most to lose but she wasn't particularly put out. The Club had to close only two short months after opening and only a few weeks after Desley had formed a partnership with her friend Sally who had opened The Dunking venue. The Dunking was closed too.

Desley welcomed the opportunity to take a rest and review everything about the club and the new venture and be ready to make any necessary changes or recommendations to Sally when they eventually reopened.

She and her partner Alvie, lived on the premises. Alvie knew about Desley's dalliances with Roger who she said she also had a soft spot for.

Desley had laughed, saying that now that they had so much time on their hands, she would endeavour to entice Roger to pop in for a threesome if Alvie didn't mind sharing. To which Alvie replied that she wanted first go.

Maria and her daughter Serina were at first, forced to stay home with grandfather Aldo and the boarder, Giorgio. They mostly worked for older people as cooks and housekeepers in the stately home of Vaucluse and Woollahra.

They successfully applied for positions with the council as carers so that they could continue working.

They both had each other and the two live-in men to play with when they felt like it plus a range of toys they enjoyed.

Maud, the owner of the music school and owner of the property at nineteen Eros Crescent found isolation difficult, severely limiting her adventures although she had managed to entertain herself with young Ashton and Damian after the two became suddenly sexually aware after falling prey to pizza nights with Jessica and Edith.

And Sylvia and Stella, the two girl who she had enjoyed briefly when they stayed over on the night of her house warming party, seducing Maude with the help their bunny outfits, had booked in for music classes and accomodation the week before lockdown. Maud reasoned that maybe life wouldn't be too bad after all.

Peoples attitudes were changed in part by the arrival of the pandemic.

Australia was fortunate that it could close its borders and clamp down easily on travel.

Europe was badly affected and Britain failed in the early stages to take action which might have prevented many of the casualties they suffered.

The USA continued to be the sad case that it had slowly become.

Big enough to make loud noises but also it seemed, too big to be able to maintain good democratic government.

It was presided over by a man who couldn't cope with an enemy he couldn't see and he couldn't lash out at, or verbally deride.

The arrival of the invisible virus was to prove his undoing.

Life on Eros Crescent went on. The residents continued to love each other in many different ways and despite the sudden disruption of the pandemic, there was a feeling of optimism in the air.

Babies were on the way and new life called out for new ideas. And new ideas about how society worked were desperately needed.

Cross your sanitised fingers everyone, and hope.

The three volumes of the Eros Crescent series are available at Amazon Books as paperbacks or Kindle ebooks.

CONTACT

Publisher or review enquiries should include your full name and details in all correspondence.

Email address:
admin@richardlee.biz

RICHARD LEE PUBLISHING

Erotic Fiction

The Eros Crescent trilogy in separate volumes - as ebooks or paperbacks:

The Fifi Code

ISBN - 978-0-909431-02-0

Eros Crescent

ISBN - 978-0-909431-05-1

Mount Eros

ISBN - 978-0-909431-08-2

Excerpts from the Eros Crescent series - as ebooks or paperbacks:

Janice: A sexual enigma

Jessica: A young woman's journey

Helen: Enough is not enough

Maria: Always available

Mary: Catching up

The Club: Ladies love it!

Literary Fiction

Australian Short Stories

Available as an ebook or a paperback.

ISBN - 978-0-909431-00-6

Restless: A novel about two young men growing up
in Australia between 1900 and 1936 (Publication date not set.)

Out of Print Titles

Mathematics for Young Children by Helen Western
ISBN - 978-0-909431-01-3

Currajong: For Those Whom Schools Have Failed
by Bruce Wicking
ISBN - 978-0-909431-03-7

The Puppetry Handbook by Anita Sinclair
ISBN - 978-0-909431-04-4

Wordswork by Chris Davidson & Bruce Wicking
ISBN - 978-0-909431-06-8

Sheep Production by Murray Elliott
ISBN - 978-0-909431-07-5

Ducks for Starters: A Practical Guide to
Backyard Duck Keeping by Bruce Wicking
ISBN - 978-1-875207-00-8

Sweethearts by Colin Talbot
ISBN - 978-1-875207-02-2

www.ingramcontent.com/pod-product-compliance
Lightning Source LLC
Chambersburg PA
CBHW030623130626
46552CB00002B/685